Sunny Side Up

MARION ROBERTS

WENDY
LAMB
BOOKS

Published by Wendy Lamb Books
an imprint of Random House Children's Books
a division of Random House, Inc.
New York

Originally published in Australia in 2008 by Allen & Unwin

Visit us on the Web! www.randomhouse.com/kids

Educators and librarians, for a variety of teaching tools, visit us at www.randomhouse.com/teachers

Library of Congress Cataloging-in-Publication Data
Roberts, Marion.
Sunny side up / Marion Roberts. — 1st American ed.
p. cm.
Summary: As the hot Australian summer draws to an end, eleven-year-old Sunny, content to be an only child with amicably divorced parents, finds her life getting much too complicated when her mother's boyfriend moves in with his two children, her best friend begins to develop an interest in boys, and she is contacted by her long-estranged grandmother.
ISBN 978-0-385-73672-5 (hc) — ISBN 978-0-385-90624-1 (lib. bdg.)
[1. Only child—Fiction. 2. Interpersonal relations—Fiction. 3. Friendship—Fiction.
4. Grandmothers—Fiction. 5. Parent and child—Fiction. 6. Australia—Fiction.]
I. Title.
PZ7.R54346Su 2009
[Fic]—dc22
2008008633

Book design by Kate Gartner

The text of this book is set in 12.5-point New Baskerville.

Printed in the United States of America

10 9 8 7 6 5 4 3 2 1

First American Edition

For Oscar

And special thanks to John, Ava, Lucian, Willow and Arthur for their unending support and inspiration

Warning! This book may contain traces of nuts.

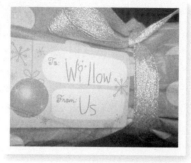

ONE

That was the summer when everything started to change, and let me tell you, change is not my strong point. For starters, Mum insisted that Carl, her boyfriend, and his kids, Lyall and Saskia, help decorate our Christmas tree. Can you imagine? Tree decorating has always been *my* job.

"I want to put the angel on," shouted Saskia, pulling a dining chair over toward the tree. Saskia is nine and Lyall is eleven.

"I'm doing the lights, then," said Lyall, taking them out of their box.

"Mind you don't get them all tangled," said Carl, giving Lyall a hand.

I gave Mum a blank stare, and raised one eyebrow as if to say *Good one, Mum. I guess that just leaves me to throw on a bit of tinsel then, fine!* I was actually a little worried about the Christmas lights. Mum said there have been cases where faulty lights set Christmas trees on fire, which you have to agree would be a total disaster, because the first thing to burn down would be all your presents.

The following week Mum invited Carl, Lyall and Saskia over for Christmas morning and present opening—without even checking with me. I mean, doesn't everyone know that Christmas is not a time to spend with people who aren't actually part of your family? It's *meant* to be just about Mum and me and Dad and Steph (my stepmother, who's going to have a baby, possibly very soon).

But this year, we all squashed into the lounge room around the tree—even our dog, Willow, who had been very naughty and already chewed the paper off two presents. She'd even eaten the cards. One of the presents was for me, from Carl. It was a T-shirt with red writing on it saying *If you can read this, you can read,* which is a lot like Carl's sense of humor.

"Do you like it?" he said as I was checking the size. "It was between that and another one which said *Smile if you're gay.*"

"Daaad-duh!" yelled Saskia, punching Carl in the arm.

"Yeah, Dad!" said Lyall. "As if she's going to want a T-shirt saying that!"

"I really like this one," I said. "Thanks, Carl." I gave him a kiss on the cheek and could smell straightaway that he'd had a cigarette, which probably explained why he and Mum had disappeared out to the shed for a while just before Dad and Steph arrived. It's also part of the reason I became a social activist and founder of Children Living with Hypocritical Parents Who Smoke. At the moment I'm the only member of the organization, but I'm sure more kids will join, because I'm not the only one living with parents who pretend not to smoke and constantly fail to give up. Seriously, my mum rings the Quitline so often they probably think she's a stalker.

Don't get me wrong about Carl. I like him, I really do—even if he is the sort of guy who wears man perfume. Carl's cool; he rides a Vespa *and* tells lots of jokes. The *only* problem with Carl (apart from his being a smoker) is that he comes with kid baggage, of the Lyall and Saskia variety. I don't exactly *not* like them, it's more that I simply don't want to see them *all the time* or have Christmas with them. Also, Lyall and Saskia argue a lot, and I'm an only child who's used to peaceful and harmonious living conditions, and I really do want to keep it that way.

Being an only child is total bliss, even though lots of people feel sorry for you or think your parents are selfish for not providing brothers and sisters. As far as I can see (and I've done my research), all siblings do is argue and bash each other and have to take turns riding in the front seat. Being an only child might have been awful if I had mean parents who locked me in a cupboard, but I have quality parents—even if they are divorced (in a friendly way). Anyway, at Mum's place we don't even have cupboards. She uses a clothing rack and still sleeps on a futon.

When I've been over at Claud's house (that's Claudia, my best friend) I sometimes come home exhausted by all the noise and fighting that goes on with her brother, Walter, who is *always* hiding the remote control and has a permanent case of head lice. And sometimes it's not just Walter and Claud. Their family does foster care, and depending on who they have staying with them, you can't be guaranteed getting a seat on the couch at all. That's when I appreciate my biffo-free conditions the most. I can lie on the couch watching any show I like, without someone changing the channel or bashing me up and infecting me with lice.

So anyway, I'm slightly off the topic now, but that's something you'd better get used to because I'm the sort of person whose mind accidentally runs off on tangents. That's why I've had to invent the Tangent Police, who are meant to step into my brain and blow a whistle if I'm off the point. In reality, though, the Tangent Police are often out on a boozy lunch, and I don't realize I'm off on a tangent until someone like Mrs. Hasslebrack (my maths teacher) sees me staring out the window and says, "Sunny Hathaway, are you paying even the *slightest* bit of attention?"

So the other totally odd thing to happen at Christmas was that Mum and I got presents from Granny Carmelene, which has absolutely *never* happened because Mum and Granny Carmelene haven't spoken to each other in about *twenty years*. Whenever I ask Mum what all the fuss is about she just gets really angry (in a silent way) and says things like: "Not all relationships necessarily last forever, Sunny," or even, "It's none of your business, Sunny. For heaven's sake, you're just like a dog with a bone." And that totally makes my throat ache.

Mum had bought some presents that I could pretend *I'd* bought for Lyall and Saskia. I (Mum) got Lyall a book about making horror movies and I (Mum) got Saskia a flower garden set. I was more excited about the present we'd wrapped up for Willow. It was a giant bone from the butcher.

"There you go, girl," I said, handing the parcel to Willow, "Merry Christmas." She took one quick sniff at the paper, then grabbed it (in a gentle greyhound way) and galloped out the back door. Willow usually buries bones straightaway, then digs them up again later. Don't ask me why. Maybe dirt gives bones an added crunch?

Dad and Steph bought me a new basketball and some basketball shoes.

"They should get you moving," Dad said, because he's what you might call *sports obsessed* and is going to be coaching our team once school goes back. I think he's planning to train us extra hard. Then he handed me the present from Granny Carmelene, and I noticed Mum's top lip go all tight and thin as I opened the card.

Dear Sunday,
    It sometimes makes me sad that we've never had a chance to get to know one another. I was thinking that it might be nice for you to come to visit me one day, if you'd like to maybe you could give me a call? I'm in the book, you know. I hope you have a lovely Christmas.
All my love,
Your grandmother,
Carmelene Aberdeen xx

Granny Carmelene had given me some posh writing paper and fifty dollars. She'd also sent photographs of her rose garden, which looked very Botanical Gardens–y, all surrounded by green spongy lawn. I reached under the tree and passed Mum the present Granny Carmelene had sent for her.

"Aren't you going to open it?" I asked.

"No, I'm not, actually," Mum said, and she stormed into the kitchen. Everyone looked at me as though it was my fault, so I followed her out there. Carl started telling a joke to smooth things over.

Mum was putting on the kettle for a cup of tea.

"I knew she'd do this," she said, banging a cup down on the bench.

"Do what? It's Christmas, Mum. It's *normal* to send presents."

"It's not normal for her."

"Well, maybe she's trying to make up."

"Well, maybe there are some things that can't be *made up for,* Sunny."

"She can't be that bad, Mum, she's your mother."

"She bloody well *can* be that bad, and the fact is, Sunny, I just want you to stay out of it. None of it concerns you. None of it."

"She's *my* grandmother," I said under my breath.

"What? No, Sunny! I know what you're thinking. You're not to have anything to do with her. Do you understand?" She opened the biscuit tin with the White Christmas slices that I'd made the day before. Willow appeared in the doorway wagging her tail. She had dirt all over her nose.

"Here, put these out for everyone, would you, please?"

"But what about—"

"Just drop it, Sunny! You're not to see her. Promise?"

I picked a bit of marshmallow out of one of the slices and put eight out on a plate, including one for

Willow, who is the sort of dog who loves White Christmas, even though sugar is meant to be bad for dogs and (according to Mum) bad for people, too.

"Sunny?" Mum said.

"Mum?" I replied.

"Promise me you won't have anything to do with her. Look me in the eye and promise."

I gave her a darting look.

"I promise," I said, hoping she wouldn't notice I had my fingers crossed.

That night I heard Mum talking on the phone to Carl. They were having the *let's all move in together* conversation again, which freaked me right out. Can you imagine? I'd have precooked siblings. We'd be one of those *modern blended families* like the Brady Bunch. But the idea of blending didn't really blend in my mind, if you know what I mean. The whole concept felt more like a murky pond with a slick of rainbow-colored oil over the surface. There're no prizes for guessing that the slick of oil, the nonblending part, was me. I wished like anything that Claud was back, because it's one thing to enjoy being an only child, but it's another thing entirely to be an only child while your bestest-ever friend is away in Queensland, and you have absolutely nobody to talk to about being forced to become *blended*. Besides, Claud and I had business responsibilities to deal with, because we're not *just* best friends, we're also entrepreneurs.

TWO

I know you can't blame *everything* on global warming, but it sure seemed as if it was around the time the massive heat wave came, and the wind grew all mad and blustery, that my whole life got blown around in circles and whipped out of shape. It was as though we were fighting a war against high temperatures, keeping all our doors and windows closed during the day to stop the hotness from stealing inside and smothering the last patches of cool. Even thinking about how hot it was makes me start to wilt, and to wonder if I can continue with this story. But I will, because I'm trying to become the sort of person who finishes what they start.

After Christmas, Mum got into a lot of gardening at night, which is how I knew she was feeling positive about life. When she lets the veggies die and the grass get wild, I can tell she's sad and feels like giving up. But Mum had been pulling weeds and planting lettuces and singing songs and watering at night, so I knew she must be feeling *up*. She was still sneaking around the side of the house to smoke, though, and still pretending she'd quit, which is the totally pathetic part of this story.

There were days when it was perfect and summery, and days when it was a bit too hot, and then there were the forty-something-degree days that made it an official heat wave. After about four days of totally mad temperatures, I started to wonder whether God might actually be bored and whether maybe we should think about getting a place in Tasmania. Somewhere inland and up high, so that we'd still have a home when Greenland melts and the sea levels rise, or if God gets *extra* bored and causes another tsunami.

I was lying on the couch, waiting for Mum to get home. We'd planned to walk to the beach together, after dinner, even though Willow couldn't come because dogs aren't allowed on the beach at night in December. I wanted to escape from the unbearableness of living in my own warm-blooded skin, so I closed my eyes and tried some creative visualization techniques. That's when you imagine things exactly the way you want them to be, and then your life is meant to just turn out that way. Don't ask me why, but

I visualized myself as a pink rubber hot-water bottle lying flat on the racks inside an empty refrigerator. I could hear the gentle fridge hum as I became colder and colder, from the outside in. The only problem was that imagining myself with cold blood led me to thinking about cold-bloodedness in general, and after a bit I was thinking of cold-bloodedness in particular.

Pretty soon I had forgotten about being a pink hot-water bottle in the refrigerator and found myself thinking about the very thing I was absolutely and undeniably afraid of, the most sinister creatures of sneakiness and cold-bloodedness, which, as far as I'm concerned, have no place of value on this earth. You guessed it. Snakes. See? Even the word *snake* doesn't sound like something you could trust. They're just so . . . *snakey.*

I closed my eyes very tightly and tried to focus on all the things that were the opposite of snakes, so I could hotfoot it right off the topic. I thought about animals with fur and pouches and big paws; animals that roll around and never squirm or hiss; animals you can snuggle up to, and ones that smell nice when they're asleep; animals with ears and cute button noses and fluffy parts that you can brush; animals that make you feel warm. But then I started feeling all warm, on top of already feeling impossibly hot, so I had to open my eyes and abandon visualizing completely.

I stood up on the couch and jumped off as far as I could into the middle of the lounge room, just in case my visualization had backfired and actually created a snake (or two) and it was waiting under the couch to lurch at my ankle. I thumped into the laundry (snakes are scared of big vibrations), took off my T-shirt, wet it in the laundry tub, wrung it out and put it back on again. This is *the* best method of cooling down if you can't actually have a swim.

I don't know why I'm so scared of snakes. I mean, they're just a tube with fangs, and most of the time they're so scared of you they slink off when they hear (feel) you coming. Only some of them chase you, like tiger snakes, for instance. . . . I think I'd better get off the topic now or I might be reminded of that old lady in Heidelberg who was innocently picking passion fruit, which she probably needed for a pavlova she was making. She was a nice old lady, the sort with blue hair and a shopping buggy, who wouldn't hurt anybody. And I could imagine her thinking pleasant, old-lady-cakey thoughts as she plucked a passion fruit from the vine on her back fence, not knowing that it was the home of a *mean* old tiger snake who bit her fair and square on her thin, veiny hand. And if it wasn't for her Jack Russell terrier, who barked and barked (as they do) until the neighbors came to see what the fuss was about—and noticed the old lady lying on the grass with just enough life left in her to tell them about the tube with fangs—if it wasn't for that incredibly loyal and yappy dog, she'd be deadibums. I don't reckon Willow would be like that, though. She'd probably catch the snake and throw it back on me, thinking it was a game of Dog, Snake and Dying Owner.

See what I mean about the tangents? According to Mum, it's because I'm an introvert. I should also mention that apart from being an introvert and an entrepreneur I'm also an inventor, a poet, a dog trainer and part owner of Pizza-A-Go-Girl, our deluxe, wood-fired, Friday-night pizza delivery service. I also like learning about psychological theories. I used to be very good at keeping secrets, but have noticed lately that I'm getting worse. Oh, and I also have the hugest collection of stripey toe socks, and my favorite dessert is baked Alaska (even though I haven't actually tried it yet).

Snakes are kind of relevant, though, because if they're not hiding under your couch they often live in holes, and that summer was making me feel all holed up, like an animal that needs to shelter all day. We'd been forced to become all indoorsy—and not the type of indoors that has air-conditioning, either, because Mum and Carl say air conditioners add to the problems we've got going with greenhouse gas.

* * *

-13

I know you're probably thinking that going for walks with your mum at night would be a dead bore, and that if I had a brother or a sister I could be making prank calls or throwing rotten tomatoes at next door's roller blind, but I like going for walks with Mum because of the conversations we have. It's true. We have really good ones when there's no one else to butt in. As long as the conversations don't involve Granny Carmelene, that is. Plus, I had arranged to meet Claud down at Elwood Beach, because she had *finally* come back from visiting her grandparents, in Queensland, who not only had a freezer in the garage *full* of Weiss bars but also took her and Walter to the Worlds (Sea World, Dreamworld and Wet'n'Wild Water World), three times. Seriously, neither of my parents has ever taken me to see any sort of attraction bigger than the Giant Worm, a place shaped like a worm, where you learn about—worms! Which is why I should report them to the Kids Help Line.

It was almost dark, and the whole of the foreshore smelt of burnt chops. The air was cooler, though, and felt like a substance you could actually breathe. There were people dotted all over the grass and the sand, and bobbing out in the water as if they were desperately waiting for a rescue mission to take them to Antarctica.

"Where did you say you'd meet Claud?" asked Mum.

"Under the tower thingy," I said, pointing to the top of the hill at Point Ormond, which was brown and dry and almost completely bald of grass.

"Poor Willow," said Mum. "You'll have to give her a big walk in the morning, before it gets too hot."

"I will," I said. "Promise!" I raced ahead of her, up to the top of the hill, because sometimes it's easier to run when hills are steep, plus it takes less time. From up top I could see right over the city. The huge scorching sun was making the mirrored skyscrapers all orange as it swooped over the sea to the horizon. It was comforting up there because not only was it breezy but I like the way life feels from above: almost as if you're looking at a map. My favorite feeling, though, is when you lean your forehead on the inside of an airplane window and peer down at the earth below. Everything becomes minute and insignificant, and trees look like florets of broccoli, and your life starts to change shape and feel like a toy life in a board game, and all your worries go away. That evening, from seat 44K of my imaginary airplane, I saw the beach as a big swirling paisley carpet. But I didn't think about it for too long because I spotted Claud jogging toward me.

She was wearing new green boardies, and her Frisbee was poking out of her bag. She's an absolutely and undeniably impressive Frisbee thrower, as well as being good at practically everything, and a tomboy in general. I, on the other hand, am a wobbly Frisbee thrower with incredibly dodgy aim, who always blames it on the wind. Luckily, I've been learning about wrist action and following through.

"Hey, Sunny!" said Claud, puffing and smiling. She was tanned and her hair was blonder. From chlorine, probably, or maybe just from being in Queensland, where the sun is a little gentler and you can actually go outside.

"Hi, Claud," I said, beaming. I really wanted to hug her but ended up just giving her a nudge with my shoulder in a leaning-in sort of a way, because Claud's not the kind of girl who's into hugging. I also wanted to avoid the situation where I was hugging her but she wasn't hugging me back. That's a bad scene. Plus, I was distracted by Mum's mobile phone ringing, and I noticed she was sitting on the bluestone wall kicking off her flip-flops and looking all smiley and girly, which meant pretty much for certain she was talking to Carl, who makes her act all teenagey sometimes because she's in love.

I was reminded of one of Carl's jokes that I wanted to tell Claud, but then I realized I'd forgotten the punch line. It's like that with jokes—I've usually forgotten the punch line before I even stop laughing. They tend to go all slippery when I try to make them stick to my memory.

Ouch! The Tangent Police just blew their whistles *really* loudly in my ear.

*   *   *

Claud and I raced each other down the hill and she beat me onto the sand, where we dumped our bags. She laughed at the T-shirt Carl gave me, but I figured it was better than one saying *Piping Hot* or *Superman* or *Roxy*, which is the sort everyone else wears and it makes you feel as ordinary as a barbecued chicken all basted and lined up at Tennyson Street Foodworks, ready to be stuffed into a silver-lined bag.

We waded into the water, being super careful not to kick any rocks disguised as sponges. As soon as it was deep enough we duck-dived and came up at exactly the same time. I kicked out to sea a bit, to make some space for a game of Frisbee.

"So how was it?" I shouted to Claud as I threw her the Frisbee, meaning Queensland in general, and the Worlds in particular.

"It was so cool," said Claud. "Even the third time." She hurled herself sideways to catch one of my wobbly throws and disappeared under the water, holding the Frisbee up above her like a trophy.

"There were these guys," Claud said when she surfaced. "I met them in the queue for the Tower of Terror, and they were sort of loser bogans, but one of them was really cute. He went on the Giant Drop with me because Walter was too scared. His name was Mitch, and we hung out for, like, the whole day. It was so cool."

"Was it really scary?"

"It was *so* scary! You drop really fast and you scream and scream. We went on it three times, then Mitch said we could go back to his resort, 'cos they were staying at Sea World Nara, and we didn't get out of the pool for, like, three hours. Seriously, it was awesome. And the next day he texted me, and we met at Wet'n'Wild and Mitch came with me on Terror Canyon Two."

"Was Walter too scared again?" I asked, practicing my wrist action.

"Nah, I just wanted to go on it with Mitch," said Claud as she lunged out wide to catch another one of my dodgy throws.

"Oh, sorry, Claud!"

"Tomorrow's going to be forty-three degrees," she said, skimming the Frisbee back to me in the straightest line possible. It caught a breath of wind and sailed above the surface of the water like a low-flying sea bird.

"I know," I said. "Not exactly *ideal* for pizza making, but it's Friday, we've got orders."

"Business is business!" said Claud.

We've got a wood-fired oven in our back shed, which is part of the reason Claud and I had the idea for Pizza-A-Go-Girl. We've got regular satisfied customers and a jar full of profits, because if there's one thing Claud and I are good at it's having ideas that work.

When it was getting so dark we could hardly see, we waded out of the water and found our towels.

"Hey, Claud? I did some more artwork for the pizza boxes while you were away."

"Great. Oh, you should see how much they charge for pizza up on the Gold Coast, and they're not even good. My grandma nearly had a fit. They charge you four dollars just for a Coke. Maybe we should put our prices up? Or maybe we should open Pizza-A-Go-Girl up there when we're a bit older."

"Pizza-A-Go-Girl goes worldwide," I said, drawing a huge circle in the sand with the edge of the Frisbee.

"I can see it now," said Claud. "Elwood, Gold Coast, Paris, New York, London—"

"And Transylvania," I said. "Don't forget Transylvania."

"Bags *not* doing home deliveries in Transylvania. Too many vampires."

"What about Rome?"

"Forget it. Too much competition," laughed Claud.

It's the fact that Claud is good at absolutely everything that makes her an ideal business partner. Not that I'm *not* good at things, but Claud is good at *different* things, and she's especially good at having conversations and making new friends. According to Mum, it's because Claud's an extrovert, which is the opposite of being an introvert like me. I read about it in one of Mum's psychology books, along with a whole lot of other interesting theories by Carl Jung (not Mum's Carl). Extroverts are chatty and outgoing and enjoy being social, whereas introverts tend to be quieter and think more. We are happier being alone, so that we can think up theories and philosophies, and read.

Maybe Claud's extrovert nature is the reason she's already into dating. But it might also be because she watches *Gossip Girl*. I don't *get* dating. I mean, why would you want to hang about with some random boy like Ivan Vandenberg? Ivan asked me to go to a movie with him once. That's how I know I'm not into dating, because I would much rather have seen the movie with Claud or even with Mum. Going on a date with Ivan Vandenberg was a big yawn. That's why I dropped him, or "nipped it in the bud," as *They* say— whoever *They* actually are. . . .

Sometimes I imagine a whole kingdom of *Theys* living in a castle in Transylvania. There is a huge stone wall with iron gates, and written in magnificent gold lettering over the spikes are the words *The Theys*. There are enormous, meandering grounds full of spooky trees infested with peacocks that shriek in the night. The *Theys* spend their day sitting around a long table, having endless banquets where *They* think up, and make official, all the things that *They* say. It's sort of like parliament, although the *Theys* are dignified and don't scream at one another or have tantrums like the politi-cians on tellie.  Once the *Theys* have come up with something new that *They* say, one of them whispers the new saying through the spiky iron gates to a town crier (who is really just a person who loves to gossip and say *Ooh aaah, you know what* They *say, blah blah blah*), and before you know it, the things *They* say are adopted worldwide. Here are a few I can remember off the top of my head:

- They say that sometimes it's best to nip things in the bud. (Which means to stop something before it starts, like dropping Ivan Vandenberg after one dud date.)
- They say you should wait for twenty minutes after eating before you swim, to avoid stomach cramps.
- They say no two snowflakes are alike.

- They say you should keep your friends close, but your enemies closer.
- They say girls' brains develop faster than boys' and that girls are better at maths (well, hello!).
- They say more people go crazy during a full moon.
- They say opposites attract (like introverts and extroverts).
- They say we only use ten percent of our brains (less in some people I know, like Buster Conroy).
- They say love makes the world go round.
- They say there's always a calm before a storm.

See what happens? There I was talking about Claud when I ended up in Transylvania in the land of the *Theys*. The Tangent Police really need to be more on the ball, I can tell you, especially with school starting next week.

Anyway, I was glad to have Claud back. Sometimes you don't realize how much you've missed something until you get it back again. I don't always like to admit that I miss people, not even to myself. But I had missed Claud a mountain. I really had.

THREE

"Sunny, wake up, darling, you've got to walk Willow. You know dogs aren't allowed on the beach after nine."

I looked over to my bedside clock. It was seven a.m.

"Mum," I mumbled, "it's holidays. I don't even get up this early on school days." I rolled onto my stomach, hoping she'd go away.

"Come on, Sunny. You agreed that if we got a dog you'd—"

"Okay, *okay*." I really didn't want to get into the *dog* argument again, because I knew what Mum was going to say and it was all true. I'd wanted a dog, I'd promised to share the responsibility and take her for walks and pick up poo from the yard.

"Well, a deal's a deal, Sunny. You promised. . . ."

I thought about leaping out of bed even though I was still feeling super drowsy, because sometimes it's easier to just gather yourself up and spring into things that you don't really want to do, so that before you know it you've already done them. Willow was sitting on my rug wagging her tail, so I had to climb down from my bunk frontward or jump right over her. If I went backward Willow would definitely shove her snout up my bum while I wasn't looking, which is just one of the many naughty things that Willow does.

Willow is a bum sniffer, it's official. And because she's a rather tall dog (and a bendy one), bums are at the same level as her long pointy greyhound snout. You see, as much as dogs can be sweet and lovely, they can also be disgusting and naughty just because they're dogs. No matter how much you train them, you really can't stop dogs being dogs. It just doesn't work.

I once tried to train Willow to be a toilet-roll holder because her snout is just the right shape for it, and I thought toilet-roll holding was a far more useful thing for her snout to be doing than sniffing bums. It was absolutely no use. She just ate the whole roll and Mum yelled at me, not just for being wasteful but because she said having a toilet roll shoved on your snout was undignified for a dog. Can you imagine? We're talking about a hound who not only rolls in rotting dead water rats but who steals dirty underwear from the laundry basket and hides it in her bed! But don't get me started, because if I was to go off on a tangent about all the disgusting and very undignified things Willow has done, it would take up the whole book. So perhaps just check at the end and I might make a list.

I raced Willow through the house, because running fast is up there with bum sniffing and dirty-underwear stealing as one of Willow's favorite things to do. She skidded on the floorboards as she ran out the back door, then did crazy ballistic laps around the clothesline before hiding behind Mum's succulent garden, thinking that because she couldn't see me, I couldn't see her crouching down in her commando pose. She had her chin on the grass and her ears flat back, and she was ready to pounce. I snuck up ever so slowly, but she leapt out at me and spun around and around on her back legs like a malfunctioning washing machine, before doing another ten laps around the clothesline.

Actually, you can hardly call it a clothesline anymore. Mum's grown wisteria all over it and now it's become a tree with curly tendrils that grab you when you run past. Mum loves it even though there's only enough hanging space left for two wet socks. She thinks it's "sculptural."

Mum was in the shed, which is where we have our

second (warm-weather) kitchen. I know it's weird, but that's just how it is in our house. When it gets cold, we

use the kitchen inside the house, which Mum says is "dysfunctional" and built for dwarves. She got so tired of bending over the itsy-bitsy little benches that she built a new kitchen in the shed using giant industrial equipment that she bought secondhand from a restaurant that went broke. The

fact is, we're tall people and we need tall benches. The shed kitchen is as big as a barn. When people come over they say they feel like they're in the country somewhere, like in Italy or France or Spain. There's a huge kidney-shaped table in the center and a wood-fired oven where you can bake twenty loaves of bread at once. There are couches around a fireplace, and piles of wood stacked up against the walls, next to all the normal stuff you keep in sheds, like pogo sticks and bicycles.

Willow raced ahead of me and jumped on the couch (naughty), panting and laughing. She really does laugh, you know. She looks half jackal and half kangaroo.

"I squeezed some fresh OJ," said Mum, pointing to a jug on the table. She was doing the crossword and flicking through the paper. I pulled up a stool next to hers so I could look at the comics and the SuperQuiz and help her with the crossword.

"What time's Claud coming?" asked Mum.

"About eight. Her mum's dropping her off before work. Hey, which British supermodel shares her surname with a nonvascular plant that grows in moist, shady areas and starts with *M*? . . . I know, don't tell me. . . . Moss, Kate Moss." I poured myself an orange juice.

"Well done. There's some fruit salad if you feel like it."

"Nah, not hungry yet, thanks, I'll have some later. According to the proverb, what makes the heart grow fonder?"

"Absence. Sunny, just stop for a minute. I need to talk to you."

"Absence is correct. Go, Mum! And don't worry, I'll do Willow. I'm just waiting for Claud to get here and we'll walk her together."

"It's not about that. It's about Carl."

"Are you dropping him?"

"Sunny, no, it's quite the opposite, actually."

"Carl's dropping you?"

"No, nobody's dropping anybody. Can we be serious for a moment, please?" Mum cleared her throat.

"Carl and I . . . well, we feel very deeply for one another, and we'd like to *share* our lives together in a more committed way and—"

"You're getting married again? How could you? You said you didn't believe in marriage."

"We're not getting married, Sunny."

"You want Carl to move in, then? It's not as if I haven't heard you talking about it."

"Well, I was going to see how the idea sat with you, Sunny. How you *felt* about it."

"What about Lyall and Saskia?"

"There's that to consider as well. When they're not at their mum's house they'd be here with Carl, and with us."

"Where? Where would they sleep?"

"They'd have the front room. Don't worry, you'd still have your own room, Sunny. No one's expecting you to share."

"But the front room's your consulting room. Where would you work from?"

"There's a room for rent in Ormond Road, with another naturopath. I could go in there. Anyway, Sunny, that's not the important part. What *is* important to me, and to Carl, of course, is that everyone feels comfortable. It'd be a big change—"

"What was the name of Norman Lindsay's Magic Pudding: Alfred, Albert or Allan?"

"Sunny, can we just finish up before Claud gets here?"

"I think it was Alfred. No, that's right, Albert. It's Albert."

"Sunny?"

"What?"

"Maybe you need time to think about it? Carl, I mean, and all of us living together?"

"I dunno. I've told you—I like Carl, but his kids are . . . well, they're *annoying*."

"Come on, don't forget you have a lot of fun together too."

"When? When would it happen?"

"Well, we thought before you all went back to school."

"Mum, that's, like, practically next week! Italian singer Luciano Pavarotti was one of the three what: basses, tenors or baritones? Oh, that's so easy, tenors, der!"

"Sunny!"

"What?"

"Yes," said Mum.

"Yes *what*?"

"Say 'yes,' *not* 'what.' "

"Why?"

"Sunny!"

"Yes."

"Can we have this conversation, please?"

"Okay. What if I said no?"

"That would be a natural response, sometimes big changes can feel threatening—"

"But would it *not* happen if I said no? Would it actually change anything?"

"Well, not necessarily. Sometimes the adults have to make the decisions, but that doesn't mean that how you feel isn't—"

"Would I have to do all the washing up?"

"Of course not, darling. We'd have to sort out a roster. You'd even have nights with no washing up." And she kissed me on the side of my forehead. "We'll talk about it more tonight. Carl's coming over with Lyall and Saskia for dinner."

"But Claud's staying over. We're making pizzas. We've got orders and deliveries."

"That can *all* still happen, Sunny. We'll make a night of it. How does that sound?"

"Map."

"Sorry?"

"Two down: Atlas, three letters. It's *map*," I said, passing Mum my glass. I was starting to feel a bit weird and in need of a little spell in the air in seat 44K to try to get some perspective.

I pressed my forehead against the coldness of the imaginary window. In seat 44K, the fact that life as you know it is about to end doesn't matter one iota. All the worry just buzzes off into the atmosphere and becomes a cloud. I imagined my thoughts being sucked into the jet engines and getting shredded into scattered solitary ideas. Up in seat 44K I get to have imaginary airplane food, which may not be made with love (according to Mum), but which is one of my favorite things on account of it all being stacked on trays in little surprise packages, like Christmas.

Willow leapt off the couch, which she wasn't meant to be on, and ran at full speed down the side of the house like a mini racehorse. She must have heard the gate open, or maybe she *smelt* Claud arriving (because dogs have supersonic noses). She ran back into the shed and hid sneakily in a corner so that when Claud came in she could pounce out and sniff her bum.

"Okay, Sunny," said Mum. "I've got to go, but I just need to say one more thing."

"Yep?"

"It's about Carl's cat, Boris. He's going to be moving in as well."

Claud parked her bike near the doorway of the shed.

"Hi, Alex," said Claud, propping her bike up on its stand.

"Morning, Claud," Mum said, grabbing her bag. "I'm just leaving. Make sure you two drink lots of water today, okay?" And she gave me another kiss goodbye.

"Hey, Claud," I said. "Which pungent edible plant is most likely to ward off a vampire?"

"Garlic!" said Claud.

"Correct. The next one's easy too. Want a juice? How many lines are there in a limerick?"

"Ah, let's see . . . ," said Claud, getting herself a glass. "A limerick? Is that like:

"Dictation dictation dictation,
Three sausages went to the station,
One got lost,
And one got squashed,
And one had a big operation?

"That's five, five lines," she said, counting on her fingers.

I checked the answers and started clapping. "Five is correct, Claud! Just look at her form, ladies and gentlemen. What a star!"

And Claud did a bow, until Willow stuck her snout fair and square up her bum.

uster Conroy is someone you're meant to feel sorry for on account of his dad being in jail and his mum having run off to Queensland to live with some man she met on the Internet. It's not like Buster's an orphan, though, because he lives with his uncle Quinny. Uncle Quinny is bald and scary-looking, but he must be sort of okay, because I see him around the neighborhood pushing a pram. I know you're meant to have compassion for people like Buster Conroy, who had to repeat prep twice and who can't actually read. But it's probably a good thing he doesn't read much, because otherwise he might end up being a bookish sort of person who might read this one day, and then I'd be dead meat.

Actually, I think it kind of makes Buster more interesting to have a dad who is a criminal, because I've got a fascination with gangsters. Not many parents at school seem to think the Conroys are so fascinating, though. No one is ever allowed to go around there for a sleepover, which probably explains why Buster hasn't got any friends, another reason I *should* feel sorry for him. But it's hard to have compassion for Buster when all he does is make me feel bad with his meanness. Not only that, Buster Conroy has a stash of BB guns that he keeps on top of the air-conditioning unit at the back of Foodworks. I know because Claud and I found them.

Claud and Willow and I were coping well with the impossibly hot weather on our early-morning walk, but we didn't count on having to deal with Buster Conroy and a stolen supermarket trolley down by the canal.

"Funny-lookin' skinny dog. What's its name, Santa's Little Helper?" snarled Buster.

I rolled my eyes backward till it hurt and said, "Yeah, good one, Buster—you're the first person to ever say that—*not!*"

Willow wagged her tail and pulled hard on the leash toward Buster, because she doesn't know there are mean people in the world. I held Willow back and tried to just walk on past, because it's best to ignore people you sense badness from, avoid eye contact and walk on by with dignity. According to Auntie Guff, my dad's sister, it also helps to imagine you're zipping all your power around yourself like an invisible fluorescent blue sleeping bag of self-protection. She says that taking notice of mean people invites their tainted energy into your auric field. It sure would have been easier if you weren't down by the canal with your best friend Claud, who happened to be an extrovert and love an argument.

Buster pushed the shopping trolley purposefully across our path.

"What's with the trolley, Buster?" Claud said. "Got a new shipment of BB guns?"

"Two words, Claud," said Buster, holding up two fingers. "Finders keepers, losers weepers."

We both laughed, and Claud said, "Ah, Buster . . . that's four words, doofus." We laughed some more, but I got nervous because if Claud kept going, Buster might get violent. When Buster gets really mad he finds it hard to control his temper, on account of not really understanding the *use your words, not your fists* rule that most of us learnt in nursery school. Seriously, Buster goes completely nuts.

"Come on, Claud," I said quietly, starting to walk away.

"Wait," said Claud. "Hey, Buster, you would have loved it at Sea World, there was a big bald seal that looked just like you. I thought maybe you were related." Claud laughed to herself (in a fake-sounding way) and Buster pushed the shopping trolley as hard as he could toward us and let go. Luckily, shopping trolleys always have dodgy wheels. It swerved straight past and hurtled into the canal, which was low in water but high in stinky mud. Then he turned and bolted down a bluestone laneway at the back of Ruskin Street. The very laneway where a dead body was found last winter. Mum tried to keep it all *hush-hush*, but everybody at school was talking about the dead woman and how she could have been murdered. . . . Sorry . . . tangent! But no wonder a violent tangent came up with Buster around.

All we could see was Buster's peroxide blond Mohawk bobbing up and down like a bunny's tail before he turned around briefly to give us the finger. Claud shouted something about Buster being in for it with the Chinese lady who owns Foodworks. Then she said something even dumber along the lines of, "We'll get you, Buster. We know where you live!"

Claud was all puffed up and exhilarated, as though she'd just come off a ride at Luna Park. I was relieved that none of Buster Conroy's badness had tainted my aura and that my sleeping bag of self-protection still seemed to be intact. It was making me way too hot though, even if it was imaginary, so I unzipped it and let it fall away.

"We've got three orders tonight," I said, changing the topic to Pizza-A-Go-Girl.

"Yeah? Who?" asked Claud, still panting.

"The Ferdinands, the Larkins and a new lady from around the corner, Mrs. Wolverine. She saw our poster down at the school. Carl and his kids are also coming over, but you can still stay the night if you want to."

"Sweet," said Claud, but she seemed to be thinking about something else.

Just when I thought our Buster-ness was done for the day, we crossed over Barkly Street and bumped into (not in a shopping trolley sort of way) Buster Conroy's uncle Quinny sitting outside Jerry's Milkbar with his pram.

"Well, well, well," said Uncle Quinny. "If it isn't Arthur and Martha. Hot enough for ya, girls?"

Before I could find my sleeping bag of self-protection again, Claud had started up a chat and was peering inside the pram at Chester, Uncle Quinny's baby boy.

"We must be crazy," said Claud, giving the pram a gentle shake, " 'cos we'll have our heads in the oven later. We're on pizza duty. Does Chester ever actually wake up?"

"Only all bloody night, the little pest. Yeah, I heard about your pizzas. You girls deliver, do ya? Don't s'pose you could get over our way? Got the boys comin' round tonight. Bit of a *card* game. A pizza or two wouldn't go astray. Heard yours are better than Shaggy's."

"That's 'cos ours are wood fired, and we don't use

shredded ham," said Claud, not picking up on any of my *LET'S GET OUT OF HERE* vibes, which I thought were pretty easy to read. I mean, you'd think after our run-in with Buster, she wouldn't want to talk pizza with his uncle Quinny. But no, the more dangerous it was, the more Claud seemed to like it. I think *They* call it pushing the envelope.

"Plus," said Claud, perching herself on a chair, "our pizzas are biodynamic."

"Listen, love, I couldn't give a rat's about bio-dynamic this and organic-shmorganic that. . . . Can I put an order in for tonight or what? I want hot salami, I mean the real hot stuff, and olives and mushrooms. Three of 'em. Big ones."

Uncle Quinny looked over to where I was standing with Willow in a wedge of shade near the café door.

"What's *your* problem, sunshine? We got a deal or haven't we? It's not bloody rocket surgery."

Uncle Quinny's head was breaking out into little beads of sweat as he stirred two lumps of sugar into his coffee. Claud was tapping her foot and giving me *the eyebrow,* looking at me like the whole thing was mine to decide.

"Business is business," I said. "Three hot salamis with olives and mushrooms." And I gave *the eyebrow* back to Claud. "Why not?"

"Eight-thirty, then," said Uncle Quinny, reaching into his shiny track pants for some small change.

"Hold yer horses, I forgot Buster. Better make that four. He'll have a Hawaiian, bloody wimp can't handle hot salami."

"We just saw Buster down at the canal," said Claud.

"Oh yeah, causing bloody trouble again, was he?"

"Well—" I said, before Claud interrupted.

"What Sunny's trying to say is that if Buster gives us any trouble, we'll spit in his pizza." Which really wasn't what I'd been trying to say at all.

"He being a bloody bully again? Damn kid, I already told him—no more bullying or he'll get a kick in the pants. Now look, I can't hang around entertaining you two all day, I got things to do, people to see. You know where we are? It's flat seventy-seven, on the seventh floor. Buzz on the door and I'll send Buster down with some cash. Got it?"

"Easy," said Claud. But I was feeling *un*easy on account of Buster maybe getting a kick in the pants from Uncle Quinny because of us saying he'd been a bully. And then us maybe getting a kick in the pants from Buster for telling tales. That's how it works, you know. *They* call it the pecking order.

"And while you're at it, have a pizza or two yourself, Sunny. You and that dog of yours both need a damn good feed. Look at your bloody canary legs, jeez!"

He banged his empty cup down and left some coins on the table, then took off down Barkly Street with the pram, making screechy bird noises and laughing to himself.

The thing is, I do have skinny legs, and they're too long as well. But Uncle Quinny calling me Canary Legs made my throat ache, even though I knew it was meant to be a friendly sort of a joke.

"Well, now what?" I said to Claud as we were crossing Marine Parade. Willow was pulling hard on the leash, knowing she'd soon be free to run to the beach.

"Now what, what?" said Claud.

"I can't believe we've got to make Buster's dinner."

"Look, Sunny, that's four extra pizzas. Just think of the profits. We'll make double the dough, and

then . . . we'll make double the *dough*. Get it?" said Claud, punching my arm. "God, I'm funny. I'm so hilarious it's seriously scary!"

I had to laugh, even though it was a really lame joke. Sometimes they're the best sort, jokes that aren't about making fun of people or being mean about their bodies and causing their throats to ache.

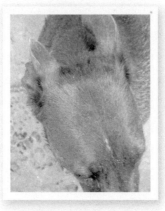

FIVE

Claud and Willow and I made a dash across the sand, which was already too hot to walk on even though it was still early. We found a cooler patch where the tide had just been.

"Race you in!" said Claud, throwing her bag down and tearing off her shirt. We all pelted into the water, even Willow, who we've been teaching to swim. She's not very good at it, though, and never goes any deeper than her neck, even when you're right there with her. I don't think greyhounds are designed to swim. She seems to think water is something to sit down in, like an elegant old lady at a hydrotherapy spa. Willow can even make sitting in a muddy puddle look good.

I duck-dived down where the world was perfect

and muffled and quiet and cool. I swam as far as I could, holding my breath with my legs fused together like a dolphin's tail. *They* say that a dolphin's skeleton is very similar to ours. Their tails are made up of two distinct bones, like human legs. Only in a dolphin the two bones become one where the ankles would be, to form the tail. I don't know whether it's just that animals seem cuter when they look like they're doing human things, but we all love dolphins because they look like they're smiling. It could just be the shape of their mouths, though. There might be no happiness behind it at all. No one seems to care about all those poor old tuna fish caught in dolphin-friendly nets and destined for a can on a super-market shelf. Maybe it's because tuna fish have downturned mouths and look slightly grumpy. Maybe I'd even like tubes with fangs if they smiled? But then again, a smiling snake would probably look rather smug, and can we just get off the whole snake topic once and for all now, please?

I made it thirty meters dolphin style underwater. At least, that's what Claud said when I came up for air. I wanted to believe her, because that would mean I had broken my personal record of twenty-five meters, so I didn't ask how she worked it out.

Willow had taken off after a Staffy-terrier, which I've noticed are a breed of dog that seem to actually *enjoy* being chewed around the neck and wrestled to the ground. It was lying on its back and wagging its tail so fast it looked like it didn't have a tail at all.

The sea was still, like a pond, and silver. I was thinking about how the air was heating up and how we had to go down Carlisle Street for pizza ingredients, and maybe even fit in a game of street poetry and another swim before firing up the pizza oven. And, of course, there was also the dinner with Mum and Carl and Lyall and Saskia to talk all about blending, which I was doing my best *not* to think about. I hadn't even told Claud.

"We got wood for tonight?" Claud asked, dog-paddling toward me.

"Yep, plenty. Mum's been dragging home old Christmas trees for kindling too, so we're all sorted."

Mum's always scavenging for wood and shoving sticks into the back of her car for the oven. Once I even heard some kids at school saying they thought Mum might be a witch, but in a good way.

I looked over to Willow, who was still wrestling with the Staffy. The owner looked toward me with an *I think your dog might be trying to eat my dog* sort of look on her face. Sometimes dog play can seem violent, but I tell you, it's what dogs like to do because they're dogs. It's just that greyhounds have a bad reputation on account of what people see them doing to those mechanical rabbits on the racetrack. But really they would have to be one of the sweetest breeds around.

I skipped out of the water toward Willow. I wanted to avoid a situation like the time when a nosy man with two demon-eyed huskies gave me and Mum a lecture about how greyhounds are meant to be on leashes at all times—even though Willow wasn't even wrestling his dogs or doing anything wrong.

"And another thing, that dog should be wearing a muzzle," the man had said, and Mum replied, "Oh really? Perhaps you could do with a muzzle yourself."

Claud and I washed the sand off our feet at the tap near the sailing club and made our way home. It was still a couple of degrees cooler inside the house due to it being made of double brick, which takes a long time to heat up. Willow slurped up half a bowl of water, then collapsed in the shade of the fig tree. Claud and I put our feet up on opposite ends of the couch in the darkened lounge room.

"Man, it's so hot you could fry an egg on the pavement," said Claud.

"I can't believe you had to stir Buster up like that, Claud. Why couldn't you just ignore him?"

"Have you ever tried it, Sunny?"

"Ignoring Buster? Yes, it's amazingly simple, actually."

"No, I mean seeing if an egg *will* actually fry on the pavement?"

"Like I care, Claud! It's too hot. Obviously the heat has scrambled your brain."

"Aw, come on, Sunny, Buster's harmless. Besides, it's fun. He's so easy to wind up. Got any eggs?"

"There's some in the shed fridge. *I'm* going to write a shopping list, because, in case you haven't noticed, Claud, we've got *work* we have to do. You know . . . eight pizzas, one hundred and twenty bucks?"

"Whoa! We've never hit the hundred-dollar mark before," said Claud.

And I said, "We're not going to make anything without ingredients."

And Claud said, "You've got to take time to smell the roses too, you know, Sunny."

And I said, "Well, you shouldn't count your chickens before they hatch, Claud."

And Claud said, "You're right—chickens mean eggs, and *do* eggs actually fry on the pavement on a hot day, Sunny? I ask you. I'll be back in a minute." And she sprang off the couch and ran out the back door.

I got out my new notebook and pens, because I'm a list-making sort of a person. Besides, when you're feeling oh-so-lazy in the middle of a heat wave, list making can really inspire you. I divided the page into

two sections: one for things we had to get down in
Carlisle Street, and the other for things we needed to
pilfer from Mum's garden.

From Carlisle St.

More eggs (now)
Hot salami - the really hot stuff
Pancetta
Pineapple
Mushrooms
Olives
Red peppers
Pine nuts
Pumpkin
Buffalo mozzarella
Ricotta cheese
Anchovies
Peaches
White chocolate
Broccoli
Red chili
Garlic
Onion
Olive oil
Fennel seeds

From Mum's garden
Cherry tomatoes
Rosemary, Thyme, Basil
Parsley
Arugula

Claud returned with the profit jar, which we hide up the back of the shed fridge. She also had the shopping buggy.

"It's like *MythBusters*," she said.

"What is?"

"The egg. This will prove it once and for all. Hey, do we need more flour and yeast?"

"Nup, we've still got plenty. Let's get going."

As I opened the front gate I saw Claud's egg experiment. She'd cracked it open right in the middle of the path, where anybody coming to our house would have to step over it. I gave her *the eyebrow.*

"It was the best spot," said Claud. "It needs to get full sun. Have faith, Sunny, faith. I think it's even starting to cook. Look, it's sunny-side up, just how you like it."

I leant over the egg to examine the edges. So far, it wasn't exactly *frying,* but I didn't want to be the sort of person who would make up their mind about something before giving it a go, so I just steered the shopping buggy around the egg and we set off for Ripponlea Station, plastering on sunscreen along the way.

I know I'm complaining about the weather a lot, but it *was* extraordinary. I guess I didn't think global warming was going to happen so quickly, even though Carl's always talking about it. I once saw some polar bears on the tellie that had drowned because they had to swim and swim in search of their icy homes, which had melted away. It not only made my throat ache, it made me straight-out cry and feel dead anxious about the future.

I also remembered that I hadn't eaten breakfast and I was feeling very *hangry*, which is what you feel when you're so hungry it makes you slightly angry. (*Hangry* isn't really my word, it's one that Carl invented and lets me borrow.)

I tried to think of a situation that was worse than mine, because there always *is* one. After all, being a bit hot and hangry isn't exactly the end of the world, even if global warming is going to destroy life as we know it. I mean, imagine what it must be like to live somewhere like Dubai, where it's about forty-four degrees every day for months on end. Or imagine being a racehorse jockey who has to sit in saunas for hours and be hot and hangry on a daily basis just to stay super thin. Or imagine being the horse!

We walked down Carlisle Street to the deli and ate nearly a whole loaf of shiny braided egg bread while we did our shopping. It was soft and baby-yellow-delicious and freshly baked on Fridays for Jewish families to share at dinner after the blessing. I know because Monica Steinberg is Jewish and she invited me to her house for Friday-night dinner once. But that was before Friday nights became Pizza-A-Go-Girl's main earner.

We parked our buggy in the last smidgen of shade outside the juice bar. Claud ordered a couple of smoothies, and I opened to a new page in my notebook for a game of street poetry. It's a game Mum invented, and we've got a street poem on our kitchen wall that she made in a marketplace in India. Claud and I have a whole book of poems we've been collecting. Street poetry is kind of like bird-watching, but far less boring. And it doesn't actually involve birds. It's more like *word*-watching. It's good when you don't feel like talking because it's all about *listening* and writing words down, one phrase at a time, from people passing by. You can only take *one* phrase from any one person, and you have to get as many as you can in three minutes. Then you arrange all the random phrases so they tell a story about where you are. Lately Claud and I have been practicing haiku, which are short Japanese poems with very particular rules. They are all about descriptions of everyday ordinariness, and the seasons. Apparently, when you get really good at haiku they become philosophical, which is why we want to practice them.

I didn't want to actually *talk* about any of the things that were weighing on my mind, mostly because it was just way too hot. I didn't want to tell Claud how Mum and Carl were planning to blend us by force. And I didn't want to explain how rude I felt for not thanking Granny Carmelene for her Christmas present because I promised Mum that I wouldn't contact her; or how unfair it feels not be able to have a grandmother in the first place, especially one who *seems* nice; or about how when Lyall and Saskia move in, I'm not going to be an only child anymore; or how it's not just the climate that's changing but also everything in my whole life, even Claud herself; and about how I wanted to know why everything can't just stay as it is. The only type of change *I'm* interested in is a cool change.

CARLISLE STREET HEAT WAVE

≈≈

FOUR HAIKU

BY
SUNNY & CLAUD

DO YOU HAVE AIR-CON?
NO, JUST A CRAP CEILING FAN
SNORING ALL NIGHT LONG

LET'S GO GET A JUICE
FEEL SO DRIED OUT, LIKE A PRUNE
WITH NO ONE WATCHING

CAN'T BEAR THE OFFICE
I HAVE THIS PINK UMBRELLA
DEEP UNDER A ROCK

STAYING AT THE BEACH
LIKE IN THE TWO-DOLLAR SHOP
I FORGET MYSELF

When we got home, Claud's egg had actually cooked on the pavement. Well, the white part had, anyway. The yolk was taking a bit longer. I ran to get Mum's camera, in case we ever needed proof, and caught Mum smoking a cigarette in the shed. She quickly butted it out and pretended she was doing dishes.

This is the sort of behavior that drove me to form Children Living with Hypocritical Parents Who Smoke. If you don't know what a hypocrite is, just ask my mum.

"Mum, it's completely obvious," I said, looking up at the smoke milling around the ceiling.

"What's going on with that egg, Sunny? I nearly stepped in it," she said, filling up the sink with water.

"How could you want to breathe in smoke when it's so hot?"

"I'm not perfect, sweetheart. Nobody is."

"Yes you are, you're a perfect hypocrite. How can you be a naturopath and smoke? It's just plain wrong, Mum."

She swung around and glared at me. "Don't you dare tell anybody, Sunny. Besides, I told you I'm going to get hypnotized. I'm on a waiting list."

"You've been on a waiting list for practically my whole life."

"Don't start, Sunny. It's a dull argument," said Mum, pulling on rubber gloves.

"Yeah right, Mum, like lung cancer isn't dull and chemotherapy isn't dull and sneaking around the side of the house to smoke isn't dull and being a stinky addict isn't dull and—"

"Enough, Sunday! Surely you've got something better to do than to harass your mother? If you're looking for a job there's a pile of dishes here."

"Can I borrow your camera?"

"It's in my bag," said Mum, nodding toward the table. "And don't you dare touch my cigarettes!"

I used to steal Mum's cigarettes and break them in half. Sometimes I'd even pour water on them, 'cos once I found her smoking the broken bits I'd put in the bin. But I gave up on confiscation because she gets really angry and just buys more and hides them. I wouldn't be surprised if she has a stash buried out in the garden. Maybe that's what she's really up to while pretending to be gardening at night?

I'm also totally over listening to all of Mum's excuses, especially the bit about being brainwashed by the glamour ads in the seventies with supermodels on yachts or the Marlboro Man or some guy called Paul Hogan who said *Anyhow, have a Winfield.*

But this is the best bit: Mum told me that in the nineteen forties and fifties young people were *expected* to smoke and girls even had smoking lessons at school. They were taught things like how to light a cigarette and how to let someone else light it for you. Can you imagine? It makes me wonder what we might be learning nowadays in school that people are going to look back on and shake their heads and say *Oh my God, they actually told kids that maths was important. What were they thinking?*

But you'd have to agree, a smoking naturopath is about as wrong-town as you can get. Why is it taking her so long to get to hypnosis? I mean, I know a lot of people are scared of it because of all those stories you hear about hypnosis turning you into a chicken, but I think Mum's just putting it off so that she can smoke for a bit longer. And I'm not buying this *waiting list* business. It just doesn't wash, which is why I end up getting so angry and wanting to do radical things like the Greenpeace activists do.

By the way, in case you're wondering what happened to the Tangent Police—I just sacked them. There was nobody down at headquarters (typical), so I just stuck a Post-it note on the door. That should do it.

Dear Tangent Police,
Sorry, it's just not working.
Don't bother coming back!
From Sunny Hathaway
P.S would you mind returning the whistles? They were kind of expensive.

Anyway, Claud and I spent the rest of the afternoon wearing wet clothing to cool down, while doing prep (that's chef talk for *preparation*) for Pizza-A-Go-Girl. It must have been about fifty degrees in the shed. We had everything stacked in square containers in the fridge ready to go, just like they do in real pizza shops. Then we made a quadruple batch of dough and left it to rise in a big metal bowl. Claud screwed up balls of newspaper and piled them onto the floor of the pizza oven dome, and I stacked a pointy pile of kindling on top, then some bigger pieces of wood, so we were ready to light the fire. Mum came out to supervise while I held a match to a corner of newspaper at one edge of the pile. Flames whooshed up toward the metal flue, making a whirring hum as the fire took off.

"I'll build up the fire for you," said Mum, "if you want to go for another swim."

"Thanks, Mum," I said, and we got on our bikes and headed for the beach.

arl was out in the shed when we got home, but there was no sign of Lyall and Saskia or Mum and Willow.

"They're at the shops," said Carl, "getting some ice cream for later."

I felt happy and hurt at the same time. Happy at the thought of ice cream, but hurt because Mum never bought it just for me, only when Lyall and Saskia came to visit. It's as if I'm not good enough for ice cream just on my own, or as if she cares more about impressing Lyall and Saskia than she does about impressing me. Any minute now she'll be making baked Alaska for them, which I can tell you right now will be the moment I run away with one of those sticks over my shoulder and a spotted scarf tied around the end containing all my possessions. You know, like Snoopy in Peanuts.

The oven was glowing with red embers, and Carl asked whether he should put another couple of logs on.

"Sure," I said. "Then we need to push the fire across to one side with the rake."

I remembered the blending talk, and felt a bit hopeful, 'cos surely Mum and Carl weren't going to launch into a totally cringe-worthy discussion right when I've got a friend over? Still, I was feeling dead uncomfortable, especially as I didn't know whether Mum had told Carl that she'd told me, or whether Lyall and Saskia knew and what they thought about it. There was so much not-knowingness in the room I may as well have been in maths.

Willow ran into the shed, wagging her tail, followed by Lyall and Saskia and Mum, who had changed her outfit and had her boobs all squashed together and dished up in a push-up bra.

"Hi. What's the deal with the egg on the footpath?" asked Lyall, putting the ice cream in the freezer. "And is there anything, like, to drink?"

"How about some, like, water, Lyall?" mocked Carl. "And do you think you can say, like, a whole sentence, like, without, like, saying *like* every second word?"

"Dad-duh! Don't be so mean," said Saskia. "Hi, Sunny. Hi, Claud. What's with the egg?"

"It's an experiment," said Claud. "We proved it was so hot today you could fry an egg on the pavement."

"Oh . . . Was that, like, um . . . I mean, was that an important experiment or anything?" asked Saskia sheepishly.

And I said, *"Why?"*

And Lyall said, "Like, 'cos Willow just *ate* it."

See? Siblings wreck your things, even if it is by accident. It reminded me of the time Walter let Claud's entire family of sea monkeys die when she went away for a weekend. Imagine the damage Lyall and Saskia could do to business. That's why, no matter how much Mum says I should be kind and let them join in, Lyall and Saskia will have to be kept well away from Pizza-A-Go-Girl.

Lyall and Saskia look nothing like one another, but I know for a fact they both have the same parents and that neither of them was adopted. Lyall is long and bendy-looking and has a rubbery face, like Carl, which makes the things he says seem funnier. Saskia, on the other hand, is more sturdy-looking and usually dead serious. They both go to the local Catholic school, which is why Saskia is going to classes to learn how to marry Jesus and why she says grace in Italian.

Mum and Carl were working on the crossword Mum had started that morning. I just wanted to make our pizzas and get out of there, in case the *blending talk* actually happened and Mum and Carl asked us all about how we *feel*, which, you've got to admit, would be dead cringe-worthy. When people ask me about my *feelings,* I just go numb and red and forget how to make words or feel anything at all.

And then, right when Claud and I were dividing up the pizza dough into neat lines of small floury balls, right when Lyall and Saskia were arguing about who was going to help, and right when Mum had just got the answer for eighteen across, Carl blurted out:

"Well, isn't this something? Why don't we do this all the time?"

And Saskia said, "What? Make pizzas?"

And Carl said, "Did you hear the one about the blind skunk?"

And Lyall said, "Daaad-duh, we've heard that one, like, a thousand times-suh."

And Claud said, "I haven't."

And Carl said, "It fell in love with a fart."

And Saskia said, "Daaaaad-duh! That joke is so lame!" and punched him hard in the arm and rolled her eyes.

But I laughed and laughed, even though it was

pretty dorky, and so did Mum and Claud because we hadn't heard it before.

And then Mum came out with, "We've been thinking—"

And Carl put his arm around Mum and took over like it was something they'd prepared earlier and said, "We've been thinking, and I'm sorry, Claud, because this doesn't really concern you, but—"

And then, without even looking up from the crossword, Mum said, "We thought it might be nice if we all moved in together . . . *here*. What do you think?"

Everybody stopped in their tracks, as if the music had just gone off in a game of Statues. I held my breath, hoping someone else would say something— anything—to break the silence and allow my lungs to work again.

Then Mum said, "Six down. *Earthenware*. Ten letters. It's *terra-cotta*."

And Carl said, "Nice one, darl. How about a vodka tonic?"

I slid the Larkins' second pizza off the peel (that's the professional term for those pizza-oven shovels) and into the box, where Claud cut it into quarters with the wheelie pizza cutter. The Larkins are vegetarians and live over the road. They were having one pizza with broccoli, fennel, garlic, chili and lemon, and one with onion, buffalo mozzarella, rosemary, thyme and cherry tomatoes, which is a combination that Claud and I saw in a book about Naples, where pizzas were invented. Claud did the delivery while I got started on the order for the Ferdinands, who live next door.

The Reverend Ferdinand and his wife, Josephine, are more adventurous than they sound. They always leave the order up to us, and the stranger the combinations, the happier they are. I guess being a reverend and living such a pure and polite life, the mystery of a Friday-night pizza is the one way they can really break out. Mrs. Wolverine round in Scott Street was having a pizza with pancetta, spinach, pine nuts, ricotta, garlic and nutmeg. Then there was Uncle Quinny's plain old hot salami with olives and mushrooms and Buster's Hawaiian, which was our last delivery before we could come home to count our profits and do our book-work.

You know, sliding a pizza off the end of a pizza peel into a wood-fired oven is all about wrist action, a bit like Frisbee. If you flick too hard it can slide too far toward the fire, and if the shovel isn't floured enough the dough sticks to the peel while all the topping flies off and ends up sizzling on the oven floor. It's all about the perfect amount of flour on the peel, and the perfect type of wrist action. Getting it right makes you feel dead powerful. I imagined our pizza business really taking off. Every Friday night we'd make hundreds of pizzas, and we'd have Pizza-A-Go-Girl T-shirts and our own delivery guy who could take Carl's Vespa, or ride a bicycle if he wasn't old enough. And there'd be people to wash up and chop and take orders while Claud and I worked the oven, thought of exciting new combinations and counted all the money. I have to say, though, that because there's only one pizza peel and Pizza-A-Go-Girl is ultimately my invention, the shoveling job would still be mine. I know that thinking about having a worldwide business possibly makes me a capitalist, but when you're an inventor *and* an entrepreneur it's sometimes hard to have ideas that *don't* make money. I mean, wait until street poetry takes off. Besides, I'm going to be the sort  of capitalist who shares a lot of money around in ways that make the world better, like finding new homes for polar bears.

laud and I locked our bikes outside Quinny's apartment block on Marine Parade. I had the pizzas tied to my pack rack with ockie straps, which I think is short for *octopus* because of the way they stretch out and latch on to things. It was twenty-five minutes past eight, so we were almost perfectly on time, which is important in a business like ours and important for me because, as I may have mentioned, I'm an *on-time* person. A swarm of leathery bikers sped past on lowriders with big handlebars. Then a convoy of bogans in hotted-up Commodores roared by. We could hear Kylie Minogue playing very loudly from a balcony.

I was thinking about the peach and white-chocolate pizza that I was going to make when I got home . . . with ice cream on top. (That's if Mum had stopped Lyall and Saskia from eating it all while we were gone.)

Claud pressed the buzzer of number 77.

"Yo!" It was Uncle Quinny through the intercom. "I'll send Buster down—*Buster!* Get down there, would ya?" he yelled. "How much do we owe yers?"

"They're fifteen dollars each," I said, leaning into the speaker.

"Jeez, you women make things bloody complicated. I didn't ask how much it cost for *one,* I asked how much we bloody owe ya.—Where's that kid?—*Buster! I said get here!*—You still there, Canary Legs?"

"Um, yes, Quinny. It's sixty dollars."

"Right, so why didn't you just bloody say that? Listen, love, you'll have to bring 'em up. Buster's gone AWOL. I'll kick his bloody behind. Push the door, seventh floor, turn left."

Claud pushed the door open, and I really wished we *had* spat in their pizzas after all, on account of Uncle Quinny calling me Canary Legs twice in one day. The foyer was hot and airless and smelt like fish fingers.

When we got out of the elevator Uncle Quinny was standing in the doorway of his flat wearing his shiny track pants with no shirt. He looked muscly like Popeye—I think 'cos he works out at the gym in case he ever gets in a fight, which he probably does all the time. We handed Quinny the pizzas and he beckoned us with his head.

"Come through, girls, the boys are just gettin' the cash together."

Claud and I stood in Quinny's entrance hall. There was a television blaring in the lounge room, where I could see the back of Buster's head on a huge curvy couch. He was playing Grand Theft Auto and was in the process of carving up a police bike with a chain saw, which is probably why he couldn't hear Quinny when he called him. There was a woman lying next to him with a sarong tied around her. She was asleep. Quinny plonked Buster's pizza on the glass coffee table in front of him.

"Nah, nah, don't get up, Your Highness, don't you move a bloody muscle!" Quinny joked. Buster didn't notice. Quinny gave him a clip across the back of the head, saying, "Where's your bloody manners, kid?"

"Hey, Buster, I *told* you we knew where you lived," Claud said, and did the fake laugh again, looking at me to laugh along. To be honest, I really couldn't see what the joke was, especially as Buster could lose his temper any moment and we weren't exactly in a position of power, being stuck in a flat full of criminals. I just wanted to get out of there.

"Come with me, Sunshine," said Quinny, moving into the kitchen. "Hey, boys, give us sixty, would ya?" he shouted. There were three men sitting around the table playing cards. One was wearing a suit like a real estate agent and sitting in front of an electric fan. There was another guy wearing boxer shorts and an undershirt, and a younger dude in a wool ski hat and a full, shiny black tracksuit with white stripes down the sleeves, as if he was smack in the middle of winter. He took some money out of the middle of the table and handed me three folded twenty-dollar notes while Quinny opened the pizza boxes and put them on the table.

"If they're any good, we'll order some more next week," said Quinny. I could hear Claud fake laughing again from the lounge room.

"Well, you better beat it, then, girls," Quinny said, standing by the door.

"Okay, thanks, Quinny. Have a good weekend," I said, putting the money in my pocket. He left me at the door and went back to the kitchen.

"Come on, Claud," I said, but she was still talking to Buster and looked as if she'd been caught doing something she didn't want me to see. "Are you coming, Claud?" I said, a little louder.

She turned around quickly, flicking her hair over her shoulder, and said, "Hope you enjoy your pizza, Buster. I don't *think* I remember spitting in it, but you can't be sure!" And then she did the fake laugh. *Again.*

"Whatever," snarled Buster, trying not to smile.

                    * * *

We waited a long time for the elevator to come. It
seemed to be stuck on the twelfth floor. Claud kept
jiggling the down button and singing "Funkytown,"
which was super annoying and made me feel like I
wasn't even there.

Just as the elevator doors were closing, the man
from Uncle Quinny's who was wearing the beanie
squeezed himself through. He was carrying a Puma
bag. Claud pressed the button for the ground floor.
She was still singing "Funkytown," which was really
embarrassing, even if it was just in front of some
stranger who was wearing a ski hat on a forty-
something-degree night and was staring at the ceiling and whistling.

Claud and I had a record-breaking night at Pizza-A-
Go-Girl, but something still wasn't right. Claud was
bouncing around like Tigger from the Hundred-Acre
Wood and kept humming and singing annoying
songs like you do when no one else is around, or
you're in the shower. And whenever I said anything
to her I could tell she wasn't really listening.

"How much of a loser is Buster?" I said, when Claud
and I were chatting in my bunks. "I mean, could he
wear any *more* Lynx? It almost gave me a headache."

"It's better than having BO. At least he cares about
personal hygiene," said Claud.

"Yeah, but he never *does* anything. I bet you he stays on that couch in front of his PlayStation all weekend. It's no wonder he doesn't have any friends."

Claud didn't answer.

"Claud?" I said, but she didn't answer me, again. "Claud?" I leant over the side of my bed to the bottom bunk. She was listening to her iPod.

"Claud!" I said loudly. She pulled out one of her earphones.

"What?" she said, in an impatient way.

"What are you doing?"

"Um, let me see, I'm making a ham sandwich. No, I'm doing my homework. What does it *look like* I'm doing, Sunny?"

"You don't have to be *mean.*"

"Well, maybe *you're* being mean," Claud said, putting the earphone back in, which made my throat ache.

"Fine. I'll turn out the light, then," I said, flicking off the lamp. I waited a few seconds. "Night, Claud," I said, but she didn't answer.

NINE

I woke up and leant over the side of my bunk. Claud was already up, I could hear her chatting to Mum in the indoor kitchen. I leapt out of bed, hoping I hadn't missed out on anything like pancakes.

"Here she is," said Mum. "Morning, sleepyhead."

"Morning," I said, rubbing my eyes. Willow sat tall in front of me, thumping her tail against the floor. Claud was already dressed and had her backpack on. She smiled at me and said, "I gotta go."

"Weren't we going to shoot some hoops?" I said. "We've got time before Dad comes."

"Nah, I've got to get home. I forgot, Mum's taking me shopping. Gotta get some new school shoes for Monday." Claud looked at her watch. "Oops,

I'm actually running late. Thanks for the sleep-over, Alex."

"Any time, Claud, you're always welcome," said Mum as Claud made her way down the hall.

"Bye, Sunny," Claud shouted over her shoulder. "See you at school on Monday!" I held Willow's collar to stop her from running after Claud.

"Claud's gone weird," I said to Willow, rubbing her ears. "Don't *you* go weird, Willow."

While I was waiting for Dad and Steph to pick me up, I dug my schoolbag out of the cupboard and tried on my school shoes. They still fitted. Dad was running late, and although I was trying to make all sorts of excuses for him, like perhaps Steph had morning sickness again, it was pretty normal for Dad to be running late because he's officially a *late person*. You'd think I'd know it by now and make internal adjustments, the way you change the clocks for daylight savings, but I always forget, because I'm absolutely and undeniably an *on-time* person and am chronically bad at waiting.

Waiting makes me itchy and twitchy and I pace up and down as if I'm in prison. Even if you have a lot of things you could do while you're waiting, it's as if the waiting itself makes you forget them all. Waiting makes me feel like I'm a puppet lying in a heap, hoping someone will come and pull my strings. Sometimes I feel like the only on-time person in the whole world. Even the cool change was late and hadn't come through in the night the way it was meant to. It was as hot inside the house as it was outside.

So I lay on the bottom bunk for a while and thought about all the different kinds of waiting and how some of them are worse than others. Like waiting for Christmas, for instance, which is almost fun because the more you wait, the more exciting it gets. Especially if you've got a chocolate Advent calendar and can possibly resist opening all the little windows and eating all the chocolates in one day. Waiting for something that is running late—like your dad, or a train, or a cool change—is a different sort of waiting, though, on account of the lateness taking complete control of your life.

Waiting for an important letter to arrive can be exhilarating but torturous at the same time, like when you enter a competition and don't know whether or not you've won. Waiting for Steph's baby to arrive is delicious, especially since the longer we wait, the more we get to feel it kick.

I wondered how long I'd have to wait for Claud to become normal again and start behaving the way a best friend should.

Dad's sister, Auntie Guff, does a lot of waiting. She's waiting to meet *the one* and fall in love. She never seems to get tired of waiting either, because she says she's got full faith in the forces of the universe. Steph wants her to try speed dating because she says a woman's got to take control of her own life, but Auntie Guff says that control is just an illusion and that everything happens in its own perfect time frame.

I think I agree with Steph, though. If Auntie Guff tried speed dating it would at least fill in time while she's waiting for the universe to get it together.

Waiting for the anaesthetic to wear off after you've had a filling at the dentist is sort of fun because your face feels all thick, and if you try to drink a glass of water, you spill it down your front.

Obviously, the Tangent Police got my Post-it-note message. It may have been a mistake to sack them!

"Muuuuum!" I shouted, putting on my new basketball shoes.

"Don't yell, Sunny!" Mum yelled from the lounge room, where she was reading the Saturday papers.

"When Dad comes," I said, "tell him I'm down at the school playing basketball. He can pick me up from there," I said, standing at the lounge room door.

"Okay," said Mum. "Well, give me a kiss, because I won't see you for the weekend." I leant over the couch and kissed her on the cheek. The good news was she didn't even pong of smoke.

"Also, Sunny, Carl doesn't have his kids this

weekend, so we thought it might be a good chance for him to bring some of his furniture over from the flat, you know, just to get Lyall and Saskia sorted and their bunks set up."

"Yep," I said, "fine by me," which was a *total* lie. I was so glad to be going to Dad's, where I could eat Coco Pops and not have to deal with Carl and Lyall and Saskia. Dad's place was starting to feel like home base in a game I couldn't get out of, where all the rules had changed.

When I got around the corner into Scott Street I could hear the sounds of basketball bouncing coming from the school courts, which was good because even though shooting goals is something you can do all by yourself, it's better when there are other people to join in with, especially when you're wanting to test out new shoes.

But something stopped me dead in my tracks. It was the sound of Claud's fake laughter. At first I thought I must be imagining things, because how could it be Claud when she had gone shopping with her mum? But then I heard it again. I hid behind the corner and peered around the wall toward the basketball courts. I could see two people, and one of them was definitely Claud. The other one was absolutely and undeniably Buster Conroy!

Even though my legs wanted to run away, my eyes

couldn't stop watching them. Claud was teaching Buster the rules and all the moves and they were bouncing the ball and laughing like old friends. I wanted to vomit and cry at the same time. How did this happen? Maybe Claud was on her way home and Buster captured her and forced her into it? Maybe he threatened to rearrange her face? Maybe Claud's mum had canceled the shopping trip and Claud was near the school when her mum rang and she just thought she'd shoot a few hoops and then, *whoosh,* Buster jumped out from behind the water fountains and she couldn't get away and she thought it was better to play along with it to protect herself. Maybe she was going to call me right afterward and tell me what a complete and utter *loser* Buster was, and how we were never going to do another delivery to the Conroys' again.

Or maybe Claud and Buster arranged to meet down at the hoops while they were talking last night, and maybe Claud didn't want me to join in so she lied about going shopping, and maybe ever since meeting that Mitch dude at the Worlds Claud had developed a *thing* for bogans?

On the way to Dad and Steph's I sent Claud a text, asking how the *shopping* was going. She texted back that she was at Smiggle and they were having a bumper sale.

Dad and Steph have air-conditioning because they're not as obsessed with the environment as Mum and Carl are, which is why I guess it's a good thing that everyone ended up getting divorced and meeting new people and matching up better, even if it does mean all the kids have to live in two houses.

I was hanging out for a bowl of Coco Pops. I stared into the pantry cupboard. All I could see were neat rows of tuna in cans. Steph was perched on the edge of her stool at the bench. It looked as if her baby bump had grown even more and was making it hard for her to breathe. Dad was brewing a pot of herbal tea.

"What's the deal with the Old Mother Hubbard situation you've got going in the really tragic cupboard?" I asked. "Where's all the *stuff* gone?" By *stuff* I meant things like Kingston biscuits and Tim Tams and all the other yummy things Steph's been having monster cravings for.

"Pregnancy-induced diabetes," said Steph. "I just got the test results back. I can't have any sugar until after the baby's born. They found too much glucose in my blood."

I pulled open the fridge. There was a plate of hard-boiled eggs, half a roast chicken and two tubs of sprouts. I checked the freezer. No ice cream.

"What the—"

"I have to do a blood test after every meal," said Steph, sipping her tea.

"The Coco Pops?" I said, looking at Dad kind of how Willow looks at me when she's desperate for a walk.

"We're a sugar-free home for a while, Sunny. It's not going to kill us," Dad said.

"Actually," said Steph, "it's *all* refined carbohydrates, not just sugar, so no white rice, white pasta or white bread. And no juices, either. No caffeine, no soft drinks, no cordial. Oh, and no alcohol, but that won't bother you too much, Sunny."

"Nah, *none* of it bothers *me,*" I said sarcastically, pouring myself a cup of tea. "Any honey?"

"Oh, the honey's gone too," said Steph. "Sorry."

"It's just a bit of a challenge for a while, mix it up a bit, support Steph. You know how it is, Sunny, you're a team player," said Dad.

"That's just in basketball, Dad."

The fact is, I'm *not* a team player. I'm used to one-on-one. It's obvious. But everything I'd been one-on-one-ing with seemed to be disappearing. Even Coco Pops. Mum had Carl. Dad had Steph. Steph was about to get a baby. Lyall had Saskia. And Claud . . . well, Claud had gone weird, which is really just a nice way of saying she'd become a bogan-loving stinking liar. I had the most horrible feeling of *just me.* I had Willow, but being a dog, she did have limitations, even if dogs are renowned for being *man's best friend.* With my luck, she'd probably latch on to Carl. If people were designed to be *just me,* then why does most of the world revolve around people trying to couple up? Being *just me* just didn't feel right.

I made myself a chicken sandwich with some new weird bread that Steph had bought, and said with my mouth full, "I'm going to call up Granny Carmelene." Both Dad *and* Steph gave me *the eyebrow.* "I'm going to go visit her like she suggested, I don't care what Mum says. She's *my* grandmother and a blood relative. She's someone who's actually . . . mine."

At Dad and Steph's there's a basketball hoop above the garage door. Surprisingly, it hadn't even melted yet.

"Come on, layups," said Dad, tossing the ball up high. I jumped and caught it, then took a shot before I hit the ground again. I missed. I could see Steph watching through the window from the couch.

"I've decided I'm going to get all the kids on the team to call me Coach," said Dad as he tossed another layup, which I put straight through the hoop.

"Even me? It's going to be hard for me not to accidentally call you Dad." I threw the ball back to him and he started dribbling it toward the basket, ready to shoot.

"Come on! Defense, Sunny, defense—you don't need an invitation to get in there."

"Dad, it's about a hundred degrees!" I said, making a lame attempt to get the ball. He swerved and shot a goal.

Dad never lets bad weather get in the way of sport. Doing exercise together is our version of big chats. We don't actually say much, but it's the way we get along. Sports are good like that—you can bounce and shoot and pass and throw your thoughts around. I was feeling uneasy about having just called Granny Carmelene and organized to go and visit her on Sunday. Speaking to her made my heart race. Her voice sounded all smooth and proper, like the people who present classical music on the radio. It was a formal kind of conversation, kind of like talking to a teacher and suddenly feeling like I didn't have a personality. Plus, the longer I spoke with Granny Carmelene, the more I remembered the promise I'd made to Mum, and how at that moment, I was officially breaking it, even if I had made the promise with my fingers crossed. I was worried about having to keep it all a secret from Mum. But then I thought about all the secrets I have to keep *for* Mum, and keeping just one secret *from* Mum suddenly felt okay.

This is what I mean (and I know there're some I've forgotten):

- I can't tell *anybody* that Mum smokes.
- I can't tell *Carl* about how Mum rings Crossword Solutions for the answers before he comes over and then acts as if she's worked them out herself.

- I can't tell *Dad and Steph* about Carl moving in yet, don't ask me why.
- I can't tell *Carl* that Mum goes through at least ten changes of clothes before practically every one of his visits, or that her cleavage is totally due to a push-up bra.
- I can't tell *Carl* that Mum is super messy and only makes her bed or does the dishes on the days when he comes around.
- I can't tell *anybody* about how Mum does witchy spells with candles and that's why there's a burn mark on the indoor-kitchen bench.
- I can't tell *anybody* about Mum's full-moon women's group, and how they sometimes dance about with their clothes off.
- I can't tell *Carl* or *Lyall* or *Saskia* about how Willow likes to eat cats, so Boris probably won't last more than a day.
- I can't tell *anybody* that I know that Dad and Steph's baby is a girl.

See? One little secret about a visit to an old lady hardly stacks up against that, does it?

* * *

I was thinking and dribbling (the ball, that is) and bouncing and thinking and dribbling when I felt the wind change and the temperature suddenly drop. The washing on the line snapped and whipped like it was about to set sail. Dad ran over and started pulling the pegs off.

"There she blows!" he said, rolling the sheets into huge balls and piling them into the laundry basket. I felt a chill at the back of my neck, then a large wet splat on my forehead, which made me look to the sky to make sure it wasn't the kind of splat that came from a large bird. There was a blanket of dark cloud making its way overhead—the sky had changed its mind from blue to charcoal in a huge, sweeping Etch A Sketch way. The con-crete steamed with evaporating rain breathing up like a sigh. And then it

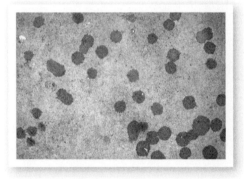

started really pelting with the cool, well-overdue, de-licious raindrops we'd all been waiting for. It was galloping down. Washing that heat wave clear out of the summer.

* * *

That night, Claud didn't call like she usually does when I'm at Dad's, which absolutely and undeniably proves she's gone weird, and is why I didn't call her either. Besides, it was the call I'd made to Granny Carmelene that I was thinking about, and I didn't even want to tell Claud about that one. Not anymore.

re you sure you don't want me to come in?" asked Dad as he pulled up outside Granny Carmelene's house.

"I'll be fine, Dad, really, and I can get the bus home too. Mum got me a new Metcard." I leant over and gave him a kiss goodbye. It was two minutes to two. I was a little (okay, very) nervous. I mean, I really knew nothing about Granny Carmelene. Apart from the fact that she used to be married to Grandpa Henry, but for some unknown reason he had gone away, and that whatever she did to Mum all those years ago caused her and Mum to be divorced, which, let's face it, *could* make her an altogether dodgy individual. The only other thing I knew was that Granny Carmelene was meant to be super posh. Dad says it's because she comes from *old money.*

Granny Carmelene's house had a huge iron gate at the front, kind of like the castle of the *Theys*. There was a smaller gate to the side with a buzzer. I pressed the button at two o'clock precisely, because being *exactly* on time really gives an on-time person an extra thrill, even if it's also completely obsessive and dorky and not the sort of thing you'd usually fess up to.

I walked up the gravel path toward the house. It was deathly quiet, except for the crunching of my shoes, which could have been mistaken for sound effects in a cheesy detective movie. I felt for a moment as though I was trespassing, or maybe being monitored by a hidden camera, which made me even more self-conscious and determined not to do anything rude, like pick my nose.

There was thick velvet lawn on either side of the path, and it circled around both sides of the house and all the way down toward the river. That lawn must have been the happiest grass ever, all plump and quenched and moist from the rain, which hadn't stopped all night. I had the urge to throw myself down and roll on it like a dog and maybe even dig a hole, because sometimes when things are so precise and symmetrical I just want to muck them up, like Miranda Percival's hair, or pictures of the Taj Mahal. There were two rounded garden beds carved into the lawn, each crowded with colored roses, like confetti.

The house was two-story with a turrety sort of tower, and was painted white with black woodwork, as if it was dressed up for something formal. A tabby cat lay asleep on a cane chair near the front door. I was twitchy and uneasy and had forgotten why I wanted to visit Granny Carmelene at all. I heard the front door open and Granny Carmelene appeared, holding out her hand.

"Sunday! How lovely," she said, smiling. The very first thing I noticed about Granny Carmelene was that she had nice teeth, but maybe they were false, because lots of old people have the kind of teeth that fall out. I was nervous about having correct manners because I heard Mum saying once that manners were more important to Granny Carmelene than love, whatever that means.

I took her hand and kissed her on the cheek, hoping I wasn't supposed to bow or something. She smelt of baby powder, which was better than smelling of mothballs like some grandparents do (usually the ones that have blue hair). Granny Carmelene was elegant and rather beautiful, in a grandmotherly sort of a way. She had long straight hair, like me, and wore it high up off her face in a silver twisty scroll. Or maybe it was a wig? You can never be sure with grandmothers, especially ones you've never met before. She wore a navy blue summery button-up dress that came down below her knees and had a wide red belt and matching shoes with square toes. She looked nothing like Mum at all, but as she turned to usher me inside I recognized that Granny Carmelene and I had the same-shaped nose as well as the same hair, just that hers was older.

"Come inside, Sunday. Let me have a look at you. Lovely and tall and shining hair, black as night. You're the picture of good health, young lady. Such a long time . . ."

I had absolutely no idea what to say to Granny Carmelene. I mean, I couldn't just come out and ask her what all the fuss with Mum was about, could I? And because that topic was forbidden, I couldn't think of anything else. I had no words and no ideas at all. Maybe my mind had fallen asleep in seat 44K and my empty body was standing in Granny Carmelene's entrance hall. It was a bad scene. For a moment I wished I was an extrovert, like Claud. She'd have been chatting away and giving Granny Carmelene compliments on her rose garden and asking her all sorts of questions, like what was the name of the cat. They'd be best friends in less than two minutes. Still, thinking about being Claud *did* help me a little.

"What's the cat called?" I asked, suddenly worried that my short-short denim skirt and stripy socks (which I'd pulled up really high) wasn't the right sort of outfit to be wearing.

"Oh, that's Marmalade. She's an old girl now, I'm afraid. Hasn't caught a mouse in years."

She led me into a dark paneled room off the entrance hall. "Here, Sunday, have a seat in the drawing room and I'll make some tea." She pointed toward a square dark green leather chair.

"Go on, make yourself at home. I won't be long."

The drawing room was dead freaky, and there were no drawings at all, just ancient-looking portraits on the walls. There was a huge one of a man with a ruddy face and a white curled wig like judges wear, and another enormous painting, in a carved gold frame above the fireplace, of a lady in a blue velvet gown standing next to a huge bowl of fruit. There were peacocks next to her, and two dogs that looked like longer versions of Willow. There were eight portraits in total. I know because, apart from being an on-timer and a list maker, I'm also a counter. The freaky part was that the old-fashioned people in the portraits were *all* staring at me as if they'd been expecting me. And freakier still was that when I edged away from the square green chair and positioned myself by the window, they were *still* looking at me. Their eyes actually followed me as if I was dead suspicious, making me feel kind of guilty. I spent a few moments looking down at my shoes (which were a bit scuffed), and then I stood over by the fireplace. When I looked up, all the sets of eyes (sixteen eyes in total) were still on me. I mean, didn't they have anything better to do? I wanted to yell out *"What?"* but was scared one of them would actually answer me. That can happen, you know. I saw it in a movie once.

I heard the whistling of a kettle and Granny Carmelene making clunking noises in the kitchen. I really hoped they were the sort of clunking noises that involved putting biscuits or cakes onto a plate, because I'm sure you'd agree I deserved some. Even if I was guilty of having an *ulterior motive.* (That's a detective term. It means looking like you're doing something for one reason but really doing it for another reason entirely, like getting to know Granny Carmelene in a long-lost-relative way while also wanting to get some *information* out of her that I couldn't get from Mum, while *also* hoping like crazy that the whole thing included cake.)

Granny Carmelene appeared at the doorway with a tea set (and cakes!) rattling about on a tray, and suggested we take it down by the river. It helped to get out of the drawing room and escape the eyes. There were steps down to a rickety old jetty and a table and chairs under the weeping willows. It was lucky for me that Granny Carmelene was the talkative type because I could only think of completely trivial things to say, as though I was about four years old. She told me that the people in the portraits were all our ancestors from England, where she grew up.

"Gosh," I said.

She poured two cups of tea. "Milk, Sunny?" she asked, holding up a matching china jug.

"Yes, please, and sugar, please."

"I made us some mini chocolate éclairs, too. Do you like them?"

"Oh yes, thank you, they look delicious. Is it real cream, like from a cow?"

"Of course, Sunday. Where else do you get cream from?"

"Well, you can get this stuff in a can now. You shake it and it comes out all whipped up," I said, sitting on one of the wooden chairs facing the river and wondering how many mini éclairs I could have before it started looking like bad manners. I had already counted six on the plate.

"Good heavens! What will they think of next?" (See, even Granny Carmelene knows about the *Theys*.)

The water was flowing fast after all the rain, and some of the ropy tendrils from the willow tree were brushing along the surface with the current. I wondered if Mum ever played Tarzan on them when she was growing up, and flung herself out into the middle of the river on hot days. I would have. I took a sip of tea and one of the éclairs, trying like anything not to ask any more dumb questions. But the more I tried *not* to, the more I seemed to burp them up like bad gas.

"Was it the English who invented hedges, Granny?"

"Do people really eat hot potato chips and butter in bread rolls over there?"

"Is it true that the Queen smokes?"

"Did you ever see any crop circles?"

"Do grown-ups really still call their parents Mummy and Daddy in England?"

"Does the Hundred-Acre Wood really exist?"

"Is it true that Christopher Robin is gay?"

"Do the English really love their pets more than their own children?"

"How far is England from Transylvania?"

"Do you believe in vampires, Granny?"

And then finally:

"Granny, why are you and Mum divorced?"

"Well, I don't really think *divorce* is the right term for it, Sunday. Do you?" Granny Carmelene sighed, and pulled her lips into a tight straight line, adjusting her belt as she stood up and stacked the dishes back onto the tray.

"Should we make our way back to the house?" she asked, without looking at me, and I realized what bad timing it was to be asking the *divorce* question when there were still four mini éclairs left. Now they would surely be packed away, or fed to Marmalade, or maybe

Granny Carmelene was planning to have them for dinner, because people who live on their own can have cake for dinner. There's no one around to tell them not to.

Because I didn't know Granny Carmelene that well, I couldn't tell how she did *angry*. Was she silent because she had nothing to say? Or was she silently angry about what I had said? If you ask me, *silent* angry is the worst. I much prefer someone to just yell at me or throw something across the room than to brood  and grump about and make the air all heavy with twisted stares and sighs. I wished like anything for the silence to go away, but couldn't think of anything to say to break it. Why did I mention the *D* word? I started finding it difficult to breathe, as if my lungs were made of thick rubber, like a whoopee cushion, that wouldn't expand.

Finally, Granny Carmelene said, "Unfortunately, Sunday, as much as your mother has many strengths, she doesn't always know what side her bread is buttered on." Which wasn't exactly the explanation I'd been looking for, I can tell you, especially as Mum doesn't even eat butter, *or* margarine, for that matter.

Still, the fact that Granny Carmelene didn't seem to be silently angry sure made it easier to breathe again. It was as if she just felt comfortable with the *spaces* between her words and didn't always hurry to chatter them in. It made more room to listen to other things, like the gush of a river after a storm and the sounds of gravelly footsteps, and the particular way Granny Carmelene brushed her shoes on the door-mat and the wiry stretching of the springs on the screen door as we went back inside.

"Come, Sunny, I'll show you the library. Do books interest you?"

I followed Granny Carmelene into a room opposite the stairs. Thank God there were no portraits. The library opened out to the front veranda, and shafts of dusty light streamed through the windows. There were bookshelves covering the walls and a ladder for reaching the higher ones. In the middle of the room was a large oval table with some old maps pinned down at the corners with glass paperweights, and some blue and pink hydrangeas in a vase. In front of the fireplace were a zebra-skin rug and two velvet armchairs, each with their own lamp. I wondered if one of the chairs had belonged to Grandpa Henry before he went away. I almost asked Granny about him, but something inside me grabbed onto the thought and stuffed it safely under a cushion.

I moved toward the table to look at the maps, and could feel Granny Carmelene hovering close behind me.

"I'm an avid collector, you know," she said, shifting the paperweights to the corners of one of the maps. "This one's only a replica, though, I'm afraid. Have you heard about the Chinese voyages of discovery in 1421? It's an absolutely fascinating piece of history."

"No, no, I haven't. But I did a project once on Christopher Columbus and how he discovered America."

"Ah yes, Columbus made some fine maps. Only now evidence suggests that it wasn't Columbus who *discovered* America at all, nor was it Cook who discovered Australia. The Chinese had already mapped it all out hundreds of years before and had circumnavigated the world *twice* almost one hundred years before Magellan. It's just that all the evidence was destroyed . . . well, almost all of it, anyway. This map, for instance, dates back to 1425. The original was found only last year in an antique bookshop in Beijing, quite by accident. The discovery of the world as we know it could be completely rewritten. It's enormously exciting, Sunday."

"That's amazing," I said, feeling dizzy, as if the swirling whirlpools on the map were pulling me in.

Kind of like an underwater version of seat 44K. Maybe there could be a submarine version, with a periscope?

"I like maps too," I said. "They make me feel peaceful, like flying, when you can look out at the map of your whole life."

She leant down to study one of them in more detail and gave a deep sigh.

"The thing is, Sunday, we all live with our pain. It becomes part of the landscape that's inside us. Your life becomes a project in cartography. You alone must map it all out. We have to become intimately familiar with what has been carved into us like a river, or laid down in us like rock. You have to find a way to flow your life around the obstacles, or through them. Or you can fence parts off, of course, but your life gets a little narrow as a result. If you spend your life shunning the painful parts, you risk them growing wild with neglect and taking you over, like weeds."

I wasn't exactly sure what Granny Carmelene was talking about. It was like listening to someone talk to themselves. I think old people do a bit of that. I moved over to the doors near the veranda and looked out to the garden. It was so peaceful, as if Granny Carmelene had created a world with only lovely things in it. She leant over the table and examined the map with a magnifying glass. Her words became soft and slow, like she was whispering into a crystal ball.

"So here we all are, Sunny, each with our joys, each with our pain. Your mother has regrets too, I'm sure. You may think pain is an obstacle, but at the core of one's pain is always a diamond. We can't change the past, my dear. But we *can* learn from it, and perhaps make different choices for the future. Grasping for happiness, I'm afraid, is like licking sweet honey from a knife."

I'm glad Granny Carmelene mentioned honey, because talking about ingredients made me feel like I had something I could add to the conversation, even though most of it sounded like gobbledy-gook to me. I mean, what did any of it have to do with Mum and the *D* word?

She looked up from the map and gave me a gentle smile, which reminded me of a sun shower, on account of a solitary tear also rolling down her cheek.

t was easy not to think about Claud's weirdness when I was at Dad's, but on the way back to Mum's on Sunday night everything came flooding back. I guess because it was Mum's place that was the scene of the crime, not to mention that I'd finally met Granny Carmelene, who had taken my mind off *everything* that I was used to, and off Claud in particular. I remembered Granny's portraits and how they made me feel as if I had done something wrong. And then I remembered that I *had* done something wrong and hoped like crazy that Mum wouldn't be able to tell that I'd broken my promise. It turned out that she wasn't in a state to notice anything much, because when I got home she was busy fussing about with Carl assembling Lyall and Saskia's bunk beds in

the front room. It was at that moment that home at Mum's stopped feeling like home. It suddenly became just a *house* with a collection of rooms to put people in.

Willow raced down the hallway, making the rug all skew-whiff. "Down, Willow," I said, trying to contain her excitement. She sat up tall in front of me. "You're a *good* girl," I said, gently pulling her ears. "Did you miss me? Did you, girl? I missed you too, 'cos you're a good good girl, yes you are, yes you are, yes you are." Willow smiled.

"Hi, darling," said Mum, poking her head out of the front room. "Come and see."

All of Mum's work things had been shifted out and Carl was stretching a fitted sheet onto the top bunk.

"Hey!" he said. "What do you think of the room? Will they like it?"

"Unlikely," I replied, before I had time to think.

"Sunny!" Mum frowned. "You could try being a little more *positive*. Look, the wardrobe fitted in after all, and Carl's even got the Internet working up here, so Lyall and Saskia can have their own computer set up."

"Brilliant," I said sarcastically. "Should I put in the order for takeaway?"

"Well . . . Carl's actually cooked one of his lovely risottos. He made fresh stock and everything."

Obviously Carl didn't know about *Sunday nights*.

Sunday nights mean Thai home delivery from the nice man Des, who used to breed greyhounds. Willow looks forward to it all week because Des whispers secrets in her ear. Once he even came in and stayed for dinner. And Sunday nights are about Mum and me and the Sunday movie, and painting our toenails on the couch, and having big chats—like the one I really wanted to have with her about school going back tomorrow, and how Claud had lied to me, and about what I could possibly do to make Claud *normal* again. Sunday nights are *not* about Carl or about Mum acting all girly over homemade risotto. Even though Carl is half Italian and probably makes a really good one.

After dinner I logged on to MSN. I really hoped Claud was online so I could let her know she was busted about pretending to go shopping, and maybe even tell her about Granny Carmelene, but, for the first time ever, Claud wasn't there.

When I got to school the next morning there was a crowd of kids around the notice board in the quadrangle jostling to see what class they were in for the year. Cecily Pritchard was crying because she wasn't in a class with Ruby Cantwell. Ruby Cantwell was standing next to Theodore Costa, who is slightly autistic and obsessed with Doctor Who. Theodore bit Ruby on the arm when he discovered he wasn't in a class with his best friend, Jet Cooper. I'd been hoping all holidays that I'd end up in the same class as Claud, but my heart sank when I actually saw our names on the same class list. Then I felt it sink some more when I saw Buster Conroy's name on the list too. There it was, in black and white.

We'd got Mr. Pratt as our class teacher. He had a comb-over hairstyle to try to disguise his bald patch. I knew Buster was already in class due to the smell of Lynx hanging about, even out by the lockers. Claud was there too, and had saved a seat for me down the back by the window. Buster was in the same row but on a table over by the door, sitting by himself with a sneery face, ignoring everyone, as usual. Mr. Pratt had only just handed out our Year Six hoodies when he gave us homework. Can you believe it? We hadn't even been there five minutes. It was fun sort of home-work, though. We had to design a house, and it didn't have to be done until after Easter.

I was uneasy sitting next to Claud, even though she was chatting away about all the things we'd usually chat about. It made my throat ache just to be near her, especially because she was saying things in an extra loud voice just so that Buster would look over at us. Then she would smile at him, and quickly turn away. *Weird!*

At lunchtime the basketball kids all ran to the court and started a game, just like usual, but this year we were king of the kids and could boss the Year Fives around. I could see Buster lurking near the water fountain, probably hoping someone would ask if he wanted to play. Claud kept checking him out, like she was sneaking a look at herself in a shop window, but pretended to ignore him at the same time. Ruby Cantwell tried for a three-pointer but completely missed the hoop. The ball flew out of the court toward Buster, who kicked it like a soccer ball as far as he possibly could in the opposite direction. Then he stormed off, nearly knocking over a Year Three kid who happened to be in his way. I raced after the ball, which I found wedged between two recycling bins near the fence. I dribbled it back to the court to find that Claud had gone. So I went too, to seat 44K.

The hostess passed me a tray of little square containers covered in foil. I curled back the foil on one to find the four mini éclairs that I didn't get to eat at Granny Carmelene's. I ate them straightaway, *before* the takeaway Thai noodles I discovered in the second silver-foiled container. The hostess offered me risotto and I said "No thanks," so she brought me some Coco Pops instead, with milk that was right at the perfect temperature.

Then another passenger sat down next to me in seat 44J. It was Claud and she was normal, like she was before she went to Queensland and discovered she liked bogans, and before she developed a fake laugh to make boys in general (and Buster in particular) notice her. It was Claud—the bestest friend a girl could have, not the type who would run off without even telling you where she was going. Better still, if she did get the urge to run, she would ask if I wanted to come too. She was the type of Claud who didn't like the smell of Lynx, and who would never make secret plans or lie—not to me, anyway, because I was her best friend and lying is just not what best friends do. If there *was* a secret plan, it would definitely include me.

I said to Claud, "Why did you say you were at Smiggle with your mum when you were actually playing basketball with Buster? Why didn't you want to play basketball with me?"

And Claud said, "Oh, Sunny, you've got it all wrong. Let me explain, I was—"

I felt a sudden hot pain as the basketball thudded into the side of my head.

"Sorry, Sunny!" said Ruby, with her hand over her mouth. "I thought you were going to catch it."

We had double maths all afternoon. Mrs. Hasslebrack told me off three times for daydreaming.

"Sunny Hathaway, whatever it is that's buzzing around in your head surely isn't maths, now, is it?"

"Sorry, Mrs. Hasslebrack," I said. I was trying to figure out what to say to Claud about her lying to me and turning weird in general. I was also thinking about my secret meeting with Granny Carmelene, and how if Claud had been normal I could have at least told one person. But every time I thought I'd worked out the perfect thing to say I found myself being whisked back to seat 44K and thinking about things like Weiss bars and noticing how whenever I thought of Granny Carmelene I felt warm.

After school Claud followed me down to the Tennyson Street shops. I was tired of worrying about what to say to her; I just wanted a Weiss bar. I had decided I definitely wasn't going to tell her about Granny Carmelene. Since she was keeping some sort of a secret from me, it was only right that I pay her back. That's just how it goes with swapping secrets.

I remembered the visualization techniques that Auntie Guff had taught me and imagined as hard as I could that it was a regular old after-school day and that Claud was her preweird, pre-bogan-loving self. But when Claud and I were down near the church, who should we see? Buster. And what was he doing? Wait for it. . . . He was down at the back of the church-yard with a bucket of hot chips, feeding them one by one to a dog through a crack in the fence and saying all this stuff to the dog in a voice I'd never heard Buster use before; you know, like a nice voice, kind of how I talk to Willow.

"Quick, hide," said Claud, pulling my sleeve. We pressed ourselves up against the redbrick wall of the church so that Buster couldn't see us behind the corner. We could hear him, though. He was having a fine old chat with that dog, telling it that he'd be back tomorrow and he hoped the dog liked tomato sauce on its chips and that next time he promised to bring it a steamed dumpling because he'd heard they're made out of cats, and that he'd do his best to get him a bone, because Uncle Quinny was going to be making a roast and even though cooked bones aren't meant to be good for dogs, Buster thought it would be better than nothing, and that he'd even try and bring him some crème caramel, because Uncle Quinny knows a really good recipe where you just add milk to the stuff from the packet. That's when Claud laughed, and not in a fake way either, her *real* laugh, like she did before she went weird. (Obviously my visualization worked.) And I couldn't help laughing too, which was when Buster heard us. Before we knew it he was standing right in front of us looking really embarrassed and really angry. I turned and made a run for it but felt a thud on my back (second thud for the day). Buster had thrown the rest of his chip bucket at me and then shot over the road toward the Laundromat. He was in such a hurry that he didn't notice he'd dropped a piece of paper from his back pocket.

Claud picked it up, and I huddled in close to see. It was a map of the streets in our neighborhood with dog names marked all over it. (In really good handwriting too, which I didn't know Buster could do. Not to mention the coloring-in!) The heading said *Dogs Need Treats* and Buster had made a color-coded key explaining what sort of dogs they were, as well as a list of all their favorite treats. There were twenty-seven dogs in total, including a schnauzer named Oscar, who lived down by the canal; two fox terriers called Maxi and Jazz; a French bulldog called Crumpet, who liked spearmint leaves; a beagle called Bruno, who liked pretzels; and a mutt called Kevin, who liked chicken nuggets from the takeaway in Ormond Road. I was glad to see Willow wasn't on the list, because we try to keep her away from junk food as much as possible.

"Cuuuute!" said Claud, and I had to agree it was, if you could get your head around it coming from Buster, that is.

As we were on our way back from the milk bar, Buster lurched out at us from the Laundromat.

"Oi," he said. "I've got one thing to say to you two."

"Don't worry," said Claud, holding out his dog map. "We won't tell anyone about your mutty little secret."

Buster grabbed the map and shoved it back in his pocket.

"It's not that, it's about Friday night at Quinny's."

"I told you," said Claud, giggling, "I'm pretty sure we *didn't* spit in your Hawaiian."

"Yeah, yeah," he said. "Listen. Firstly, you don't tell anyone what I'm about to say. Secondly, you do and I'll kill ya. Thirdly, you didn't see nothing going on at our flat. If anyone asks, like the police or anything, you didn't see nothing. Get it? Especially that guy with the ski hat, you especially didn't see *him*."

"You mean the guy with the ski hat and the Puma bag," I said.

"This is the deal, right? You bloody didn't see that guy. You didn't see him at our flat, you didn't see him in the lift and you didn't see him leaving our building. Okay? There was no guy in no ski hat."

"And with a Puma bag," I said, pulling up my socks.

"There was no guy in no ski hat, with no Puma bag, at our flat. Got it? Now beat it, I gotta pick up the washing."

"See you tomorrow, Buster," said Claud over her shoulder in a singsong voice. I think I may have even seen her wink at him, but I couldn't be sure.

"Yeah, later, Claud," Buster said with his chest all puffed out.

That night it was just Mum and I at home because, even though Carl and his kids had moved some of their things in, the blending wasn't official until

Wednesday. It was most likely going to be our last chance for one-on-one conversation before the house was totally invaded by a stepfather and precooked siblings.

Mum and I had one of our big chats. The type of chat that leaves you in a ponder afterward and makes you carve out your own opinions. I told her about Friday night at the Conroys' and about how Buster had threatened us.

"What if the police call and ask if I saw that man with the ski hat? I'd have to lie, and I don't even know why."

"Look, Sunny, I don't know what's going on over there, but don't worry about Buster. The fact is, if you *are* asked anything by the police, you'll just have to tell them exactly what you saw, the ski hat man included," said Mum.

"Really? I could still tell the truth about everything else and just leave out the bit about the guy in the ski hat. That's not technically lying."

"It is, actually," said Mum. "Truth is truth. It's an absolute, not a set of parts. Omitting part of the truth means you're automatically lying—you're manipulating the facts to suit yourself. An edited version is no longer the *absolute* truth, do you see?"

"Sort of, but I still reckon lying is saying something that isn't true, not choosing *not* to say something that *is* true."

"Put it this way, if you don't give a thorough account about everything you *did* see, *technically* you wouldn't have *told* a lie, but you'd be living a lie, and living a lie *is* lying."

"What if the consequences of telling the truth are that your life gets all messed up by Buster Conroy?"

"You can't worry about the what-ifs. Buster's probably just full of hot air anyway. The fact is, if you're asked to make a statement about what you witnessed you just have to do it, then you can deal with the consequences with a clear conscience."

"Yeah right, Mum, like the consequence of needing facial surgery?"

"Sunny, now you're being hysterical. Living an honest life doesn't always mean living a comfortable life, but it means living with integrity and honor. Telling the truth shows you have the courage to look life in the eye. Only a coward needs to lie, Sunny. Now, that's not you, is it?"

"What's for dinner? I'm starving."

"Chicken gumbo," said Mum.

All that thinking about lying, and all that chicken gumbo, made me want to lie down. Willow had snuck onto the bottom bunk in my room and was hoping I wouldn't notice if she leapt off when she heard me coming down the hall. She was standing in the middle of my bedroom looking like someone who'd been caught shoplifting. The giveaway, though, apart from the pathetic *I didn't* expression on her face, was the flattened-out warm patch she left on the duvet, right up near the pillow. But I couldn't be cross with her. She's just too cute. Besides, you should only get cross at dogs if you actually catch them in the act, which is not so easy to do with Willow, I can tell you. She's a very crafty hound.

I climbed up to the top bunk to think. The thing is, if what Mum said was true, it meant I was lying about seeing Granny Carmelene in secret. Or I was *living* a lie, at least, which amounts to the same thing. But it's not as if anyone asked me about it. I mean, if Mum had come out and asked, *Did you visit your grandmother when I told you not to?* I wouldn't have had a problem telling her, even though I knew she'd go feral. But she didn't ask me, so it was totally unfair that it meant I was a cowardly person living a lie. Why should Mum have cared anyway, given she spent most of her time pretending Granny Carmelene didn't even exist? She didn't even seem sad about it.

If you ask me, I think Mum just pretends not to care. If she didn't have emotional issues, she wouldn't have wound up addicted to smoking. Anyway, *she* could talk! How about the lie *she* was living: she was a chain-smoking naturopath!

And what about when Granny Carmelene gets really old and dies? Mum might suddenly realize she really does love her after all, and get all over-whelmed with guilt and emotion, and end up in one of those lonely wintry cemetery scenes where she's down on her knees begging forgiveness from a tombstone. It happens all the time, you know. I saw it once on TV.

arl, Lyall, Saskia and Boris officially invaded on Wednesday, right after school. Mum and Carl wanted to have a modern blended family dinner to celebrate our new togetherness. I asked if we could make baked Alaska for dessert, because so far I'd only ever seen pictures of it in *Larousse Gastronomique* (which is a cookbook that's so fat it should really think about going on a diet), but as usual Mum said it was too complicated and that it would be better to do it in the school holidays, which, of course, had just finished. Let's face it, it's *never* school holidays when I get the urge for baked Alaska.

Boris was locked in the front room as part of his settling-in process. He is a pure-black cat. They're meant to bring bad luck if you happen to see one crossing your path, but in Boris's case I think the bad luck boomeranged. For a cat like Boris, who looks *a lot* like a rabbit, winding up sharing his life with a greyhound isn't exactly *fortunate*. He was definitely lined up to become a dog's breakfast. Willow had taken up a full-time position outside Lyall and Saskia's room with her snout squeezed under the door, making loud snorting sounds and shaking all over.

We were all out in the shed kitchen waiting for Carl to come home. Mum was making a Vietnamese salad to go with barbecued fish. I was cutting potatoes into wedges and thinking about Willow and Boris, and baked Alaska, and about how my head was awfully itchy.

"They'll be fine," Mum said, peeling carrots. "They'll get used to one another. It happens all the time with dogs and cats."

"Can I help peel?" asked Saskia.

"I want to help too," said Lyall, who probably didn't really want to help at all, but didn't want to miss out on something Saskia got to do, even if it was as dull as peeling carrots. That's what siblings do, you know. It's a constant competition.

"Lyall-luh! I asked first, and anyway there's only one peeler!" roared Saskia.

"That's unfair-ruh. You always get to peel-luh."

"Well, jeez, Lyall-luh, find your *own* job-buh."

"Mum," I said, scratching my head, "I think I might have lice."

"Eeew, like, gross," said Lyall.

"No it's not. It's not my fault. The whole school's got them, Lyall. There's an epidemic."

"Not at our school," said Saskia.

And I said, "What? Catholics don't get lice?"

And Mum said, "Now, come on, you lot." (Can you believe I get referred to now as *you lot*? I used to have my own name.)

"Can you check, Mum?" I said, leaning my head toward her. "Please?"

"Sunny, it's not really the right time, darling. Can't it wait until after dinner? Lyall, how about lighting the barbecue. Do you think you can do that?"

"I want to light the barbecue!" said Saskia, throwing down the peeler and racing Lyall outside.

"On second thoughts, you guys, maybe wait till your dad gets home!" Mum shouted after them.

"Mum, I can't bear it! I need you to run through my hair with the lice comb. I can *feel* them multiplying!"

"Sunny, for God's sake! It's not all about you right now, okay? I *said* I'd do it after dinner!"

"Fine!" I said, tossing the potato wedges into a baking tray. "Be like that, then!" And I went inside and played "Greensleeves" as loud as I could on the piano, until Carl came home and asked me to stop because I was creating noise pollution.

*   *   *

After dinner, Carl suggested we have a *meeting,* so that we could all *communicate* about *issues,* like doing the dishes and getting pocket money. Carl spoke first. He started off with lightbulbs and how we need to change over to the sort that use less energy and produce less carbon dioxide, and how we should fight climate change by becoming a carbon-neutral household, and how we should think about ways to contribute to the community—like Claud's family does when they do foster care. Then he got onto the kitchen roster and showed us how he'd *rearranged* the utensil drawer.

Mum and Carl divided the kitchen jobs into three sections: clearing the table, scraping plates and com-posting; washing and drying dishes (including put-ting away); and wiping down the benches and the stove. It was starting to feel like boot camp. Back in the good old days (last week) there were just a couple of plates, the odd pot and a few pieces of cutlery to wash.

Next we talked about the issue of fruit-juice guz-zling. Mum and Carl announced that we were each to be given a two-liter bottle of juice per week, which we were to mark with our names and keep in the fridge. A permanent marker would be attached to the fridge on a piece of string. Once your bottle of juice was gone, no more would be issued until the next supermarket shop, which was to take place every Monday.

Mum gave me *the eyebrow* when I butted in with, "Jeez, Carl, what's next? Six a.m. jogs? A whiteboard with colored pens?"

Lyall and Saskia both giggled, but Carl was all straight-faced and said, "Actually, Sunny, thank you, that's not such a bad idea."

We talked about the issue of bedtime, the issue of computer usage, the issue of wet towels not drying in a heap on the floor and the issue of appropriate bathroom usage. We talked about laundry days, television usage, pet integration, dog walking, spare keys, homework, school lunches and pocket-money deductions if chores weren't done properly. I felt a bit worried for Mum—if that was the stuff she and Carl spent all their time talking about, they couldn't have much else going on. Maybe they needed a hobby? Bingo might be good.

"Well then," said Carl. "Any questions?"

"Have you got a strategy for lice epidemics, Carl?" I said.

Mum gave me the *double eyebrow*.

That got me thinking about the Transylvanian Compatibility Booth, and how Mum and Carl could sure use one. The *Theys* invented the Compatibility Booth for affairs of the heart. Everyone should have one. It's sort of like how satellite navigation devices in posh cars tell you you're going in the wrong direction.

The Transylvanian Compatibility Booth ensures you're dealing with the sort of love affair that will actually last and not the sort that looks all fine and dandy at the start, but ends up like sour cream, 'cos you're with the wrong person and have wasted a whole heap of time getting married and divorced and having kids who have to grow up in two houses. If Mum and Dad had bothered to step inside a Transylvanian Compatibility Booth they would have set off the siren of absolute incompatibility for sure. They would have had nothing at all lighting up in the Soul Mates panel and everything lighting up in the Seriously Consider Breaking Up section, as well as one very bright flashing button saying Do Not Marry, No Matter What. But then again, if Mum and Dad had used the Compatibility Booth I wouldn't be here at all, so maybe scrap that whole idea. Maybe I'm just a little bit old-fashioned.

When Mum tucked me into bed that night (after removing fifteen lice and buckets of nits from my hair), I asked her whether she thought Carl might possibly be a control freak. But she said he just likes to be organized, and that we'll live more harmoniously with his well-thought-out systems in place. I thought about Granny Carmelene and her peaceful world, which didn't resemble a boot camp at all. I could even imagine myself living there if I was forced to run away.

At least my bedroom was the same as it ever was, even if it did smell of lice shampoo.

"Night, Sunny," said Mum, kissing my forehead. "Everything's all right, you know, we're just going through a big transition. We'll all be really happy. You'll see."

"Even Willow?"

"Of course, even Willow *and* Boris. You'll see."

"Promise you won't smoke anymore, then, if you're so happy."

"Oh, that's right, I forgot to tell you. I'm off the waiting list for hypnosis. I've got an appointment!"

"Finally! Night, Mum," I said, giving her a hug and knowing that she'd be sneaking straight out to cram

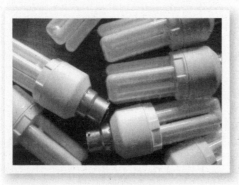 in some more cigarettes before the hypnosis removed the urge to smoke from her hard drive. If she did quit, though, I could think about resigning from Children Living with Hypocritical Parents Who Smoke, which, I must admit, was a bit of a shame, 'cos I'd secretly been looking forward to hosting a demonstration.

uster wasn't at school for the third day in a row.

"What's with that?" I asked Claud, after Mr. Pratt finished calling the roll.

"Don't know," said Claud, looking away. I noticed she had gone red.

"Have you seen him anywhere?" I asked.

"Nup," said Claud. But it felt like she was lying, because blushing is often a sign, and I'm very good at sensing things.

"Have you decided what you're going to do for your design project?" asked Claud, changing the subject.

"I thought I'd design a grand, old-fashioned mansion, with a drawing room and a turret, and a library full of books. How 'bout you?"

"Mine's a future house," said Claud. "With circular rooms, and ceilings that open up so you can sleep under the stars. You'll never guess what Buster's designing, though—a dog hotel," Claud laughed.

"I thought you said you hadn't seen him."

"I haven't," she said, blushing again. "He . . . um . . . told me on MSN."

The best part about Mrs. Hasslebrack's maths class was that it was the last class before the weekend. She wrote *BODMAS* across the board in red and then a whole lot of equations that we had to solve using the *BODMAS* rule. I like *BODMAS* because it gives you an order in which to go about things that are usually confusing, like maths. And because if you follow the *BODMAS* rule everyone comes up with the same answer, unless you totally make a mistake.

Mrs. Hasslebrack wore a girdle (Mum told me) that pulled her tummy and her bottom in at the same time and made them look really hard and flat, and exactly the same shape as one another. It made me want to poke her, just to see if the girdle tummy was actually as hard as it looked. She also looked orange because she wore too much fake tan. She handed out some sheets for homework, pausing at Buster's empty desk.

"Will anybody be seeing Buster over the weekend?"

Claud's hand shot up. "I will, Mrs. Hasslebrack. I'll see him at basketball tomorrow," she blurted out, then looked at me as if she'd seen a ghost and slid the maths sheets into her folder.

"*What?*" I exclaimed, almost so loud the whole class could hear.

"I told you," said Claud defensively, "Buster's going to try out for the team."

"You did *not* tell me, Claud! How could you?"

"Sunny Hathaway, would you *please* stop talking!" scolded Mrs. Hasslebrack. "Not *another* word!"

Boy, did seat 44K feel good for the rest of maths. I peered down at the shambled world far below, until cotton-candy clouds floated across my view. The fact that my best friend had officially fallen to the dark side didn't bother me at all. I ate a chicken sandwich with homemade mayonnaise and chives. Then I cranked back my chair and fell asleep. When I awoke, Claud was sitting next to me in 44J. She was screwing up Buster's maths sheets and talking about how much spit she was storing up for his Hawaiian that night at Pizza-A-Go-Girl.

Claud and I argued all the way through our deli shopping.

"You could have at least *asked* me, Claud," I said, ticking red pepper off the list and putting it in the buggy.

"What's the point, Sunny? You weren't going to agree. Besides, it's a community team. Buster has every right to join. You should feel sorry for him, anyway. How would you like it if your dad was in jail and your mum had disappeared?"

Claud took a fifty-dollar note from the profit jar, ready to pay.

"Yeah, like how I feel sorry for Osama bin Laden. Get a grip, Claud!"

Claud's phone beeped. She pulled it out of her pocket to look at the text message. Can you believe it? Her whole screen was lit up with a photo of Buster. What's more, in the photo he'd had his Mohawk cut off, which made me dead suspicious. It had *still been there* last time he was at school—solid evidence that Claud *had* seen him. Not only had she seen him, but she'd taken a photo of him, saved it on her phone and linked it to his number. My God!

So, even though I'm not a big fan of silent angry, I did it the whole way home. I just couldn't help it, and neither could Claud. That was why it was such a relief to find Mum and Carl out in the shed with Lyall and Saskia. Claud and I could ignore each other without it being so obvious.

The oven was already lit, and there were dead Christmas tree needles all over the floor.

"We helped get the fire going," said Lyall, and Mum looked sheepish 'cos she *knew* I didn't want Lyall and Saskia thinking they could weasel their way into Pizza-A-Go-Girl. She knew that!

"Did you see the surprise in the lounge room, Sunny?" asked Carl, winking at Mum, who was doing the crossword and making it really obvious she didn't want to look at me.

"No, what?" I asked, getting the juice marked *Sunny* out of the fridge. I didn't want to offer any to Claud, but I knew Mum would pick me up on it, so I had to do fake manners so as not to cause a scene. "You want some, Claud?"

"Sure," said Claud. I saw her do *the eyebrow* to herself when she noticed the names on the juice bottles.

"So what is it, Carl, a plasma screen?" I said. "You beauty!"

"Well, no, but it is big and flat and hangs on the wall. Go see for yourself."

I ran to the lounge room. Willow was still sitting outside Lyall and Saskia's room, drinking up the smell of Boris that was wafting under the door. She didn't even run to greet me.

There are no prizes for guessing that Carl's *surprise* wasn't a plasma screen but was of the whiteboard variety, with the dishes roster already drawn up. *What next?* I thought. *A minivan?* Claud followed me into the lounge, saw the whiteboard and looked at me blankly with an *Is he freakin' serious?* look on her silently angry face. I take back *everything* I said about thinking Carl was cool. I was obviously deluded. Or maybe that was the old Carl—the Carl who just used to visit a few times a week and tell jokes and make Mum happy, even if he was also a tragic smoker.

Apart from Uncle Quinny, who had ordered the same pizzas as the week before, all our other regular customers had left the decision making up to us. The only thing we had to remember was that the Larkins are vegetarians.

"So," I said, looking over our list of orders. "We've got Uncle Quinny's three hot salamis with olives and mushrooms, Buster's Hawaiian, pizza verde for the Larkins, pizza with artichokes for Reverend Ferdinand and pizza Sant'Agata for Mrs. Wolverine. I'll start washing the herbs."

"You sure about the Conroys' order?" asked Claud sheepishly. "I mean, did Uncle Quinny actually put an order in?"

"What do you mean?" I asked. "He told us last week that he wanted the same again. Remember? And then he left a message on Monday to confirm."

"Well, it's just that I heard he might be going away for the weekend, that's all," said Claud, getting the scales down to weigh out the flour. "Forget about it, I'll get the dough started."

Just then Claud's phone beeped again with another text message. I was leaning over the sink, so I couldn't see whether it was the sort of text message that was attached to a photo of Buster's dumb head.

"Ah—I gotta go," Claud said, looking guilty and putting her phone back in her bag.

"In your dreams, Claud. We've only just started prepping," I said, soaking the herbs in a sink of shallow water.

"Is everything all right, Claud?" Mum asked.

"Um, I think so, but Mum just wants me home right away."

"Claud! What about our orders?" I said, banging a metal bowl down on the sink. "It can't be *that* important!"

"Sorry, Sunny, I've just gotta go."

And that was that. Claud jumped on her bike and left me holding the baby (as *They* say), or in this case, holding an entire pizza delivery business. I take back what I said about Claud making the perfect business partner. That was the *old* Claud.

And I also take back what I said about not wanting any help from Lyall and Saskia, because, to be honest, they saved the day, even if it was a night. Lyall ran the Larkins' order over the road while I got going on Reverend Ferdinand's. He was back in time to deliver Mrs. Wolverine's while I got Uncle Quinny's order under way.

Saskia cut the pizzas and packed them in their boxes, as well as slicing up all the mozzarella while I made sure the oven was okay. Mum and Carl pretty much stayed out of it, because apart from being stuck on the crossword (Mum must have forgotten to call Crossword Solutions), you could tell that they were hoping Lyall and Saskia and I were *bonding,* which sort of made me cringe. But I did start to think that having precooked siblings might end up being a good thing—for business, I mean. If Pizza-A-Go-Girl did take off, Lyall and Saskia could be employees, only I wouldn't have to pay them much because they'd be family, which also meant they wouldn't be able to abandon me right in the middle of our orders.

Mum didn't want any of us going to the Conroys' on our own, and to be honest, I didn't fancy it either. (It was the first thing we'd agreed on in days.) So Carl offered to drive me there in Mum's car, and act like a delivery guy and a bodyguard.

"Hey," said Carl in the car on the way to the Conroys'. "Do you want to know what I think the best name for a pizza business is?"

"What?" I asked.

"Eureka Pizza . . . Get it? You reek *of* pizza!" which really did make me laugh, but not as much as Carl, who sometimes enjoys his own jokes more than anyone.

"I just made that up!" he said, which for some reason made me feel a little easier about the whiteboard and him being a control freak, 'cos at least he could still tell the odd joke.

Carl buzzed on the security door. I was really

hoping we wouldn't have to go upstairs this time, and that Quinny could just bring the money down and take the pizzas. There was no answer, so we buzzed again. Still no answer.

"Are you sure they were expecting pizzas, Sunny?" Carl asked. "Maybe they *did* go away for the weekend."

"Well," I said, adjusting the four pizza boxes so that my hands weren't so hot from holding them underneath. "Quinny never said anything to us about going away. Ask Mum."

Carl buzzed again, for about seven seconds (I just happened to count while I was waiting). But there was still no answer.

"Probably got the TV up loud," I said.

A man came out of the main door to the flats and saw us waiting to get in. He had fake blond bits in his hair and wore a T-shirt that was way too small.

"Who are you after?" he said to Carl.

"The Conroys," Carl replied.

"What? Quinny?" asked the man. "Didn't you hear? He got carted off by the cops. When was it? Tuesday night. Drugs, apparently. Nah, the Conroy place is all closed up. Quinny's lady took the baby and headed off to relatives in Perth, last I heard."

"What about Buster?" I asked, beginning to make sense of why he hadn't been at school.

"Gone too," he said. "Apparently staying with friends, or something, until they track down his mum."

"But Buster hasn't got any fr—"

"That'll do, Sunny," said Carl.

I was hoping he'd had to move to the other side of town—somewhere with a nicer-sounding name, like Sunshine or Deer Park, but too far away for him to be on our basketball team, or even go to our school, or bother taking Claud away from me.

When we got home, Carl put the Conroy pizzas in the

fridge for us to eat over the weekend (it was lucky I didn't end up spitting in Buster's). When Carl was making room on the top shelf, I noticed that the profit jar wasn't in the back of the fridge where we usually hide it. It was absolutely and undeniably gone. I looked everywhere. You don't have to be a genius to work out who might have taken it, given that she now hangs about with criminals' spawn.

teph's baby is a girl. But that was a big secret because Dad didn't know and wanted it to be a surprise. Steph found out at the ultrasound, and I did too, because Dad and Steph let me go with them. Dad stood outside for the part where the radiographer told us she was a girl. So there was no talking of names either, because that would be a giveaway, but Steph told me in secret that she wanted to call the baby Flora.

"Like in Babar," I said, with my hand on Steph's tummy. "Remember, Celeste had triplets? There was Flora, Alexander and Pom."

Steph said, "Exactly. Flora as in Babar."

Steph and I were lying on the couch when I felt Flora kick. You could even see it, a heel or an elbow rolling along Steph's tummy like a wave. I rested my ear near her belly button, but all I could hear was gurgling. The baby seemed to take up every bit of space.

It was hard to imagine how all the usual stuff, like Steph's liver and kidneys, could keep working properly when they were squashed up into corners. It was even harder to imagine how Flora was going to fit out. Thinking about it made me want to cross my legs.

"Are you scared?" I asked. "Of the birth, I mean."

"Not at all. I'll just turn myself inside out like a sock," said Steph.

Flora will be eleven years younger than me, which means we really won't have much to argue about. It's perfect. With an age gap that big you can pretty much guarantee she's going to idolize me. When Flora's seven, I'll have my own car, or maybe even a motorbike with a sidecar, and Flora can wear goggles and a silk scarf. I'll pick her up from school and won't get her home till late, and I'll do all her homework, and we can make baked Alaska anytime we like.

Steph asked about Pizza-A-Go-Girl. I told her about Claud nicking off, and how she'd gone weird in general, and it was even looking like she'd stolen our profits.

"That does sound weird," said Steph. "But it also sounds like you and Claud may just be growing up at different speeds. I remember when boys suddenly seemed to matter. They will to you too, Sunny, but maybe not right now, that's all."

"Did you develop a fake laugh?" I asked.

"Probably," Steph giggled.

"Did you walk funny, with your shoulders all pulled back when the boy was around, and pretend to be ignoring him? And did you treat your friends bad and leave them out?"

"Could you be jealous, perhaps, Sunny?" said Steph as she struggled to sit up. "I mean, it's normal to be jealous and all, but—I don't know how to say this— maybe you're being a little *possessive*? Maybe Claud still likes you as much as ever, but you're just not the *only one* anymore? Oh, I almost forgot, your grandmother called and wants you to ring her back. There's a message on the pad over by the phone."

I jumped up and called Granny Carmelene straightaway.

"I was thinking, Sunny," she said over the phone (after we finished saying all the polite things you say at the beginning of phone calls with posh people), "that you might like to accompany me on an outing. I have to go into town next week. Perhaps we could go together? There are some places I'd love to share with you. How does next Thursday sound?"

"It sounds fine, except for me having to go to school," I said in a hushed voice as I took the phone into my room so that Steph didn't hear.

"Good God! It won't hurt you to miss a day, surely? School takes up far too much of a child's life, if you ask me. Half the time, children learn nothing at all."

I felt like I couldn't really say *no* to Granny

Carmelene. And mostly I didn't want to say no either, so I agreed to meet her under the Flinders Street clocks on Thursday morning at ten. I figured I wouldn't really have to lie. I could just add it to the list of all the other secrets that I had to keep, which was why, by the way, I had come up with my latest invention, the Stash-O-Matic. . . .

With the Tangent Police long gone, due to absolute incompetence throughout their entire department, I needed a device that could monitor my levels of chronic secret keeping and let me know when they were getting dangerously high. The Stash-O-Matic was designed to go *ping* when my brain was in danger of bursting, to stop me from blurting out all the stored-up secrets to the wrong people. It made me think of the mean old man in Ackland Street who blurts out swear words all the time, and how a Stash-O-Matic could be just the thing to cure his Tourette's syndrome.

Steph had fallen asleep. I heard Dad coming home, so I quickly shoved the secret about next Thursday with Granny Carmelene into the top of the Stash-O-Matic and slammed the lid. According to the Stash-O-Matic, my secrecy levels were already dangerously high, so from then on I had to be sure not to shove in any new ones without getting rid of a few old ones first.

"Aha! There you are," said Dad. "Ready for the game?"

"Shhh!" I whispered, pointing to Steph. "She's asleep."

"Come on, then, get your gear, Sunny. We'll leave Steph to sleep and go a bit early for a decent warm-up."

In the car I told Dad about Buster trying out for the team, and about how nuts he gets if something makes him angry.

"I think it's a great idea," said Dad. "Team sport could be just the right medicine. Anyhow, Sunny, he'll be judged on his merits and given a fair go, just like everybody else."

That pretty much meant for certain that Buster would get in, especially as Claud had been giving him secret lessons.

"So, Carl and his kids moved in this week," Dad said. "How's it all going?"

Good one, Mum! I thought. She could at least tell me when a secret was no longer a secret. She'd specifically asked me not to tell Dad about Carl moving in.

"It's going okay, I guess. I'm a bit worried for Boris."

The first thing I saw when Dad and I arrived at the basketball stadium was Claud and Buster sitting on the bench together giggling into their Gatorade. I wondered whether Claud knew about Uncle Quinny getting arrested and Buster becoming a sort-of orphan, but I didn't wonder for too long because I couldn't even look at them, due to being so angry about everything in general, and the profit jar in particular.

Jet Cooper arrived with Alice and Ruby and Ruby's mum, who is our team manager and does the scoring. Dad got us doing some drills, and I found I could look at Claud and Buster more easily if it was about catching or throwing or bouncing a ball. I still felt awful, though. I didn't want to admit it, not even to myself, but I think I *was* dead jealous, just like Steph said, and I really didn't like the idea of being a possessive person at all. I can tell you, feeling jealous would have to be the *worst* feeling in the world. Worse than being called Canary Legs twice in one day.

Buster got so many fouls against him that Dad had to give him a good talking-to after the game about learning to control his anger—but he made the team all the same. While he was signing up, I grabbed Dad's keys and went and sat in the car so that I didn't have to talk to anybody or put on a fake nice face.

"Poor old Buster's been going through the wringer," Dad said as we were driving home.

"Yeah," I said sarcastically. "Poor old Buster."

"Lucky he doesn't have to move schools, though. And it'll do him the world of good to stay with Claud's family for a while. They'll be a really good influence. It's a great thing that they do—foster care."

"Are you freaking serious? Buster is *living* with Claud?"

That night in bed I remembered another thing that *They* say. *They* say that jealousy is a curse, which is *exactly* how it felt. Even though I was justified, I wished like anything I knew how to get the curse removed, like by visiting a witch doctor or something. I was worried that if I didn't find a cure quickly, I would have to do something drastic.

FIFTEEN

I tell you, by Thursday I really needed a day off. You try sitting next to someone you're not talking to for three whole days—it's torture. All that making sure you stare straight ahead so that you can ignore them properly is exhausting.

On Tuesday, Claud passed me a note, but I just screwed it up and put it in my mouth and chewed and chewed before spitting it in the bin in the middle of English.

"Freak!" said Claud as I sat back down.

On Wednesday, she wrote me another note, but this time she held it up in front of my face so I couldn't help reading it. It said she was coming over after school on Friday, for Pizza-A-Go-Girl. I gave Claud *the eyebrow,* as if to say *I'll believe it when I see it, Claud. Besides, I happen to have employed two reliable new workers, if you don't know, and they're not the sort to abandon me right in the middle of orders, or the sort who steal the profits.* That's why I like *the eyebrow*: there's just so much it can help you say.

On Thursday morning, Lyall and Saskia and I all left home together. It was a good thing they went to the Catholic school—that way, they wouldn't know about me wagging school to spend the day in the city with Granny Carmelene. And because they didn't know, they wouldn't be tempted to tell, or feel they had to tell a priest about it in confession.

Saskia was worried about Boris and Willow being home alone together all day, especially now that Boris was allowed outside.

"He can just jump up onto the fence again, like he did yesterday," Lyall said.

"But what if Willow chases him, and Boris runs away?"

I turned the corner as if I was heading in to school. "Boris will be fine, Saskia. See you later," I said, waving goodbye.

"Bye, Sunny," Lyall and Saskia said at the same time.

When Lyall and Saskia were out of sight I turned back and cut across the grass to the canal. I sat on the bench to eat my lunch, which was really my breakfast because I'd been in too much of a hurry to have any, due to the queue for the bathroom. Also, I figured it would be rude to eat my lunch in front of Granny Carmelene, and I didn't think she'd be that excited about sharing a vegemite sandwich and a bunch of grapes. Maybe she had plans to take me somewhere posh, like the Hotel Windsor, where we could have tiny little cakes and tea. While I ate my lunch, I thought of a new word—*jangry*. It's when you're already hangry but you're cursed with jealousy at the same time.

It was one of those perfect, gentle, summery days that aren't too hot and don't make me scared about global warming and polar bears. I lay on the cool morning grass by the canal. There were some newly hatched ducklings following their mother up toward the golf course, and a huddle of kids from the high school were smoking cigarettes under a cypress tree on the opposite side. I closed my eyes and looked up to the sky through warm purple eyelids. For a few minutes I felt completely at ease, but then I ruined it by thinking about Claud and Buster, so I stood up and set off for the station, because sometimes when you walk fast you can leave unwanted thoughts behind.

Granny Carmelene was on the steps under the clocks at Flinders Street right on ten. I could see her from behind, checking her watch as I came out of the gates. She had her hair up in a tall, twisty bun just like last time, and she wore a greenish flowery dress and pale alligator-skin shoes and carried a matching handbag.

"Hello, Granny Carmelene," I said, leaning in to give her a kiss.

"Sunday! You're right on time. I'm so glad you could come. I know it was a little inconvenient, missing school and all."

"No, I wanted to come, really," I said, just as a busker playing the bagpipes got started and made Granny Carmelene jump.

"Oh dear!" she said, looking over her shoulder at the busker. "Let's get going, I need to go to the map shop in Little Bourke Street. I'm planning a short trip to Tasmania."

We crossed over Flinders Street and made our way down Swanston Street, fighting through a stream of people coming the other way. It made me wonder why they don't have white lines down the middle of busy footpaths, just like on a road, so that people would stick to their side. But then I guess it would be hard for people to stop and look in shops if you were on the wrong side of the line. There were so many words coming out of the street, like the city had something big to say and nobody would listen. It made me think of street poetry and how a Swanston Street version would be a good one for the book. Almost every shop had a spruiker out front with a microphone. *Only ten dollars, ladies and gentlemen, ten dollars is all you'll pay, ten dollars for two . . .*

"Ghastly racket!" said Granny Carmelene, and I smiled back at her to let her know I agreed, because it was too loud to answer with words.

We cut down Royal Arcade, past the old-fashioned lolly shop, where a girl was working fast to stretch a hunk of warm yellow toffee around a hook on the wall. The more it stretched, the paler and shinier it became, until it looked like a thick strand of pearly hair that reminded me of the Rapunzel story. Granny Carmelene and I stood inside and watched her and a guy plonking and stretching and rolling the colored toffees into one another, then rolling and stretching them out again. Finally, the guy snapped hundreds of brittle hunks off with a cutter and held out a scoop of tiny sweets for us to try.

"Pesshenfruit rock?" he said with a smile, but it wasn't until I tasted it that I knew he meant *passion fruit,* and that he was from New Zealand. It really did taste like passion fruit too. Not like how chicken chips taste nothing like chicken, and barbecue chips taste nothing like chops and sausages. It made me want to try all the flavors, but I could tell Granny Carmelene was tired of standing up, so we kept going.

In Little Bourke Street, over the road from where Granny Carmelene wanted to get her map, I spotted a shop called Spellbox. Maybe they would have something to help remove my jealousy curse?

"We can have a look in there afterward, if you like," said Granny Carmelene, who must have noticed me reading the tarot signs out the front of the shop.

"Okay," I said, "if we've got time."

"We've got all the time in the world," said Granny Carmelene, holding open the door of the map shop for me.

There were all sorts of maps, for absolutely every place on earth, and lots of globes of the world too. But there was also a sign that said you weren't allowed to touch any of them or spin them around. While Granny Carmelene was in the Australian section, I tried to find a map of Transylvania, but I couldn't even find a listing for Transylvania in the European index.

"What are you looking for, Sunny?" said Granny Carmelene, appearing behind me.

"I'm trying to look up Transylvania, but I can't seem to find it anywhere," I said, running my finger down the long list of places starting with *T*.

"Are you sure you don't mean Tasmania, Sunday?" Granny Carmelene chuckled. "I'm planning a trip to Tasmania, not Transylvania. Besides, I think they call it Romania these days, dear."

"Oh," I said, feeling like I really should have known that myself, given that Transylvania was my favorite country, not to mention being the homeland of the *Theys*.

Granny Carmelene opened out a map of Tasmania and put her glasses on to have a better look. "Are you called to travel, Sunny?"

"I've been to Bali," I said. "But I was just a baby. When we finish school, Claud and I want to go to Naples, 'cos that's the home of pizza making. And I really want to go to Madagascar, 'cos that's where vanilla beans come from, and they're my favorite sort of bean. Oh, and I want to go to Disneyland, 'cos, who doesn't, really? Is this where you get your old Chinese maps from, Granny? I'd like to go to China, too."

"Good heavens, no! My maps are antiques. I have an art dealer who specializes in old maps. He's found some very rare ones and is on the lookout for me all the time. Ah, here's what I need." She pointed to a place on the map called Mole Creek. "Right here, Sunday, is where you'll find King Solomon Cave. . . . Now, did you want to look in that shop over the road?"

Granny Carmelene paid for her map and put it in her handbag, and we crossed the road to Spellbox. I could smell incense as we climbed the narrow stairs. A woman with waist-long hair and hoopy earrings smiled and said hello. I was too embarrassed to ask how to lift a curse of jealousy that caused throatache *and* heartache, so I just looked around at all the witchy things and hoped the curse-lifting section would jump out at me. Being there also made me think of Mum, and I wondered whether she knew about this shop.

I found the prepared spells section. It was full of kits and instructions. There were spells for love, for banishment, for a change in luck and for prosperity and protection, but I didn't see anything about removing a curse. There were colored candles, too, which are meant to help with stuff when you light them. I read all the labels while Granny Carmelene browsed through the books. There were yellow candles to help with study, childhood issues (whatever they are), travel and confidence. Orange was for success, which I thought might be good to burn on Pizza-A-Go-Girl nights, and blue was for healing and relaxation. There was also a completely empty box for green candles, which were supposed to help with money, fertility, luck and employment. At least I wasn't the sort of person in need of green, not that a bit of extra luck ever goes astray.

I bought an orange candle and a yellow one, and went over to where Granny Carmelene was flicking through a book.

"You know, Sunday," she said, "the women in our family have a lot of intuition. It's in the bloodline."

"Is that like being psychic?"

"It can be, but not always. You should listen to your

intuition, though, Sunday. The more you listen, the more it guides you," she said, putting the book back on the shelf. "And it's very rarely wrong."

I was worried Granny Carmelene was going to launch into one of her talks again, about things I didn't really understand. But I did understand what she meant about intuition, 'cos I get strong feelings about things, and sometimes it helps me make decisions. Like when Uncle Quinny ordered pizzas for his card game that night. I had a big bad feeling about the whole thing, and not just because we'd seen Buster down by the canal. It's pretty hard to listen to your intuition, though, with somebody like Claud around, who just says yes to everything, and a double yes to dangerous things that turn out to be a bad idea (even if they are profitable).

Granny Carmelene didn't take me to the Hotel Windsor for lunch. We went to the Hopetoun Tea Rooms in the Block Arcade instead, and we walked over thousands and thousands of minuscule tiles that made up the mosaic floor. The window of the Hopetoun Tea Rooms was full of old-fashioned cakes—like pavlovas and lamingtons—and inside there were tea sets for sale in all shapes and sizes, even one in the shape of a cat. There was a strange cash register that swiveled around. A waiter showed us over to a marble-topped table near the wall.

"On the topic of mosaics," said Granny Carmelene

as we sat down, "I went to the most wonderful cathedral once. It was in Sicily, and the whole of the interior was covered in mosaic tiles depicting the stories of the Old Testament. The floors, the walls, even the ceiling. It was just marvelous! If you ever get a chance

to go, Sunday . . . Are you hungry?"

"Very," I said, even though it wasn't really true because I'd already eaten my lunch for breakfast. I had a look at the menu.

"What's Welsh rarebit?" I asked. "Is it really rabbit?"

"No, no," Granny Carmelene chuckled, "it's a type of mustardy cheese on toast."

They had other strange things on the menu, like pinwheels, which sounded sharp, as if they might get stuck in my throat. So, because the waiter was standing there and looking impatient, I quickly ordered some chicken sandwiches with crispy bacon and mango mayonnaise. Granny Carmelene chose a sandwich with red salmon and cucumber, as well as a pot of tea.

There were a lot of grannies at the Hopetoun Tea

Rooms, as if it was the cool spot for grannies to go. Most of them had blue hair and wore pastel blue and pink, like babies' clothes. I was glad my granny Carmelene didn't dress like a baby; she looked more like someone all dressed up for the Melbourne Cup.

"You know, Sunny," she said, after the waiter delivered our sandwiches, "there is something important I need to tell you, but you must promise me to keep it to yourself. I've not told anyone at all."

Like I needed *another* secret! The Stash-O-Matic started humming even before Granny Carmelene told me her secret, because it has sensors that tell when a new one is hovering about.

Granny poured her tea slowly through the strainer and stirred in some milk. I didn't tell her about all the other secrets I was keeping, or how I'd had to invent the Stash-O-Matic to manage them all, because even if you are completely full of secrets it's still very exciting when someone gives you one more—especially one that absolutely nobody else knows about, and even more especially if you think it might be the big big secret about Mum and Granny Carmelene's divorce.

"I'm good at keeping secrets," I said as I bit into my sandwich, which was cold, obviously from having spent time prepared in a fridge.

"Well, dear, I don't want you to get upset," she said, placing the teaspoon carefully on her saucer. "This is very difficult to say. . . . It's about my health. I have what you might call *a condition*."

"Like a disease?" I asked, feeling my stomach tighten.

"It's called CLL, Sunday. Chronic lymphocytic leukemia. It's a cancer of the blood."

"But . . . can't you get better? Claud's auntie had cancer and got skinny and bald and everything, but now she's fine and the cancer's gone away. Can't there be a cure?"

"There's treatment, Sunday, but no cure, I'm afraid. Besides, I'm not interested in becoming skinny and bald. There's no dignity in that at all."

"But—"

"Sunday, I know you might not understand, but it's my choice to accept my time when it comes and pass gracefully when I'm called to go. It's a decision I've made. Now, you must promise not to breathe a word of this, especially not to your mother."

I didn't feel like the rest of my sandwich. All I could think about was Mum, and how if she knew Granny Carmelene was sick and dying she mightn't be so stubborn and angry toward her, and how the hugeness of Granny's secret was causing the Stash-O-Matic to *ping* loudly. I thought of Claud, and I suddenly realized I wasn't angry anymore, or even jealous. It was like the news about Granny Carmelene's illness had broken the curse. I could feel my eyes welling up and wanting to cry, so I looked down at the curly parsley on my plate, hoping that if I concentrated really hard, I could make the crying stop. Let's face it, breaking into a blub in front of someone you've only met once before would be dead embarrassing.

"Come now, Sunny," said Granny Carmelene, reaching over to hold my hand. "I've lived with this for many years now, and I intend to keep on living for as long as I can. Life is so precious—sometimes it's only when you know it might be taken away that you can begin to really appreciate it. I feel quite liberated, to be honest. There's nothing at all to fear, don't you worry."

"Aren't you scared, Granny?"

"Of dying? Not at all. I'm more scared of not living. I intend to live and live, until I'm asked to let living go. And now that you're here to share some of my living, Sunday, I feel happier than ever. It's all just perfectly marvelous."

It didn't feel so marvelous to me. I mean, you wouldn't read about it (except that you are): you find your long-lost relative only to discover she's got cancer of the blood. It was enough to put me off having any pavlova, even though I knew I'd be missing out on a chance to sneak some sugar without Mum telling me it's bad, or Dad and Steph reminding me it's banned. Then I thought of that old lady and the snake again and wondered whether, if it *was* your turn to die, it might be better to just pop off with a bite to the hand while picking a passion fruit.

"Sunny?" said Granny Carmelene, who must have sensed I was off on a tangent. "You know that cave I told you about, in Tasmania?"

"King—?"

"Yes, that's the one. King Solomon Cave. I went there once as a girl, and I've never forgotten. For some reason, I just have to go back. It's my intuition, Sunday. Have you ever been inside a cave? This one is over twenty million years old. Can you believe it?"

"I find caves a bit freaky, actually," I said, happy that the topic change had made my tears go away.

"Well, I think you'd be surprised at just how majestic a cave can be. Will you come with me to Tasmania? We'll go for a weekend and I'll show you. Do tell me you'll come, Sunday."

t was a bit tense that night at dinner. Carl and Lyall had been arguing about Lyall forgetting to put the bins out that morning, and when people argue it makes me feel uneasy, as if it might all be my fault, even though I know it isn't.

"It was up on the whiteboard, Lyall, there's no excuse," said Carl. "Now we're going to have stinking rubbish hanging around all week long."

"Yeah, Lyall," said Saskia, "you should have to do the dishes tonight all by yourself. Shouldn't he, Dad?"

"That's enough from you, miss," Carl said, spooning some brussels sprouts onto Saskia's plate.

"Dad-duh! You know I hate brussels sprouts, they look like green sparrows with no heads and legs-uh!"

"Please stop whining, Saskia," said Carl.

"Yeah, Saskia," said Lyall, and he punched her arm.

Mum had the look she gets when her nerves are jangled—her lips were all thin. She was probably having a craving because she'd started hypnosis and hadn't had a cigarette in three days.

"Come on, everyone," she said. "Let's just enjoy our meal. Sunny, would you pass the salad, please?"

And I said, "Sure." But what I really wanted to say was *Sure, and if you care at all, your mother's dying and I said I'd go to Tasmania with her for a weekend, if that's okay with you.*

I mean, the thing is, I really did want to go to King Solomon Cave with Granny Carmelene, even though I didn't like the idea of being underground. I'd even done some research on the Net and read about how a farmer had discovered the cave back in the nineteen twenties when his dog was chasing a wallaby. The wallaby disappeared down a hole, which turned out to be an entrance dropping nine meters below the surface to the cave. I also looked up CLL, which was totally depressing because there's not much hope for you if you're an old lady with cancer of the blood. Especially when you're the sort of old lady who thinks medical treatment is undignified and doesn't believe in drugs.

"What is it, Sunny? You look miles away," said Mum. "And you haven't touched your chicken."

"I'm just not that hungry, thanks, Mum," I said, pushing the food around my plate.

"Did you hear the one about the cat who swallowed the ball of wool?" said Carl, trying to improve the mood. Lyall and Saskia rolled their eyes.

"She had mittens!" said Carl. "Or how about this one? Why don't cannibals like eating comedians?"

"Daad-uh!" squealed Saskia. "Would you just stop?"

"Because they taste funny!" giggled Carl.

We all laughed too, except for Lyall, who said, with a deadpan face, "Dad, that's not funny, that's just lame," and he started clearing the plates so that we could wash up.

Just then there was a sudden yelp from Willow and she ran into the shed with her tail between her legs and Boris chasing close behind. Boris was all puffed up with his ears down flat. Willow cowered in a corner as Boris growled and closed in on her with sideways steps. Then Boris flung himself at Willow—just like one of those gliding marsupials. Willow let out another yelp as Boris hissed and scratched her on the face three times; then Boris bolted outside and jumped up onto the fence. Willow burrowed into the couch and curled into a ball with her head hidden between the cushions.

"Did you see that?" laughed Lyall. "Go, Boris!"

"Yay, Boris!" shrieked Saskia. "You show 'em, Boris!"

Mum and Carl looked around in a daze. "Can I get you a vodka, darl?" Carl asked.

"Perhaps a peppermint tea," said Mum, tight-lipped.

I gave Willow a big hug. She had a deep scratch right across the end of her nose. There was even blood. She was shaking and crying in a dog way, which doesn't involve tears or making noises, but just looking up sorrowfully and showing the whites of her eyes.

"Poor Willow," I whispered in her ear. "Boris is a mean, mean cat, and we're going to make him pay."

While we were washing up, Saskia told me that she had put a Pizza-A-Go-Girl poster up at her school and that she was pretty sure one of their teachers would be putting in an order for Friday night.

"It's Father Kenny," she said. "He's our parish priest. He loves pizza."

"Aren't priests meant to eat fish on Fridays?" I asked.

"That's only in Lent," said Lyall, wiping down the sink.

"Okay, bring it on," I said. "We'll deliver to anyone: criminals, priests, who's next?"

Willow slept in my room that night so that she could stay well clear of Boris. I thought about Granny Carmelene all alone in her big old white and black house. Maybe if Mum gave her another chance, she'd find that Granny Carmelene had changed. People do change, you know. *They* call it *mellowing*. And anyway, what was there *not* to like about Granny Carmelene? Even though I'd promised that I wouldn't tell anyone about her illness, I couldn't help thinking that if Mum *knew,* it might make her forget about whatever went on in the past. And how could I go away for a whole weekend without Mum knowing where I was going? Maybe I could just let Mum think I was at Dad's, and let Dad think I was at Mum's. There had to be some advantages to having divorced parents. I could become *invisible* and slip off to Tasmania without anybody noticing. I'd have to hope like crazy that neither of my parents called the other one to talk about anything normal, like basketball. I'd be living a double lie, with double secrets on top. Imagine what that would do to the Stash-O-Matic! It would probably blow the whole thing up.

But I had to go to Tasmania with Granny Carmelene, not just because she was dying, but because I wanted to *live* and have adventures and get out of doing the dishes, as well as have a big dose of good old-fashioned one-on-one. I wanted to see King Solomon Cave with my own blood relative, even if her blood was faulty. I just *had* to go, my intuition told me. Surely I could live a double lie (and possibly break a perfectly good Stash-O-Matic) . . . just once?

laud *did* turn up for Pizza-A-Go-Girl on Friday night, even though I didn't really want her to. And we *did* get an order from Father Kenny, as well as two other new customers who were friends of Mrs. Wolverine's. Saskia was reading the pizza dough recipe and measuring out some yeast into the scales. She'd also been working on some new pizza box labels, which I had to say were better than the ones Claud and I had made, because Saskia is *really* good at art.

"I can do all the deliveries," said Lyall. "But can't we change the business name to something not so *girly?*"

Claud must have overheard him from the backyard.

"Sorry, Lyall," she said as she came through the shed door, "Pizza-A-Go-Girl has a solid market reputation. It would be bad for business to change names now." She gave me *the eyebrow,* as if to say *Back me up here, Sunny.*

"I agree," I said flatly as I put another log on the fire in the pizza oven.

"Me too," said Saskia. "So you're outvoted, Lyall. Besides, I've already designed our Pizza-A-Go-Girl T-shirts."

"There's like, *no way* I'm wearing a Pizza-A-Go-Girl T-shirt," said Lyall just as Mum and Carl came into the shed with herbs from the garden.

"Mmm-mm," said Carl, "fresh basil!" And then he started dancing around the shed with it, singing that old Dean Martin song about the moon hitting your eye with a big pizza pie. Then he sang his own version— *"When you eat tuna fish on a big silver dish, that's a mornay"*—until Lyall and Saskia begged him to stop.

"Dad, you're embarrassing us," said Saskia under her breath.

"Claud, you're here. Great! How are things at home?" asked Mum. "Is Buster okay?"

"Pretty good, thanks," said Claud. "Still no word from his mum, though," she said, looking at the list of orders I had made, and I said, "Yeah, well, you *would* nick off, wouldn't you? If you ended up with a kid like Buster."

"*Sunny!*" just about everybody yelled.

"It wouldn't hurt to have a little more compassion," added Mum.

"Yeah, Sunny," said Claud. "Get over it!"

"*You* get over it, Claud!"

"Hey, I've an idea!" Lyall interrupted. "How 'bout Buster joins the business too? Then I wouldn't be so outnumbered by girls."

"Now, there's a thought," said Carl, washing the herbs.

And Mum said, "That's a good idea, Lyall."

Even Saskia said, "I don't mind."

I was the *only* one who said, "Noooooooooooo!"

"What is your *problem,* Sunny?" said Claud.

"My problem? *My* problem? I'm not the one who's gone *weird,* Claud. You're the one who has a complete personality change the minute *some boy* is around. I'm not the one who *pretends* to be doing stuff they're not. I'm not the one who laughs fake. I'm certainly not the one who doesn't bother to tell important stuff— like Buster joining *our* basketball team. And I'm not the one who stole the profit jar, Claud, I mean, that's sinking pretty low!"

"What!" yelled Claud. "How can you say—"

"Wait a minute," said Lyall. "That was me. I mean, I didn't steal it. I moved it to inside the piano. I thought it would be safer and then I, like, forgot all about it. Sorry! I'll grab it," he said, running out of the shed.

"Sunny," said Mum, shaking her head, "what's got into you? You didn't really think Claud would steal." She was frantically looking through a pile of newspapers for the crossword.

"Listen, Sunny," said Claud. "There're things you don't know. I *couldn't* say anything about Buster because we were chosen as his foster family and there are privacy rules and all this stuff that you're not allowed to say. That's why I couldn't stop you making up Quinny's pizza order last week, even though I knew he wouldn't be there. And as for basketball, it was Mum who suggested that Buster should try out, and I had to take home his homework sheets, 'cos he was staying at our place."

"Sunny, you didn't burn *today's* paper, did you? I can't find the crossword," said Mum.

"Got it!" puffed Lyall, running in with the profit jar.

"And anyway, Sunny," added Claud, helping Mum sort through the papers, "sometimes you're not the easiest friend to have either! Sometimes I don't want to do *everything* together. Sometimes I want to have other friends too. I mean, can't you just *share*, Sunny? You know, like, just *share*?"

Claud turned to Mum with a crossword from last week's paper and said, "How about this one, Alex? It's not done yet."

But Mum just looked stressed and a bit mad, partly

due to not smoking and partly due to the fact that she had probably already memorized the answers to today's crosswords from calling Crossword Solutions, and was hoping to look impressive in front of Carl. Last week's crossword just wasn't going to cut it.

Just then Carl walked in with a ladder and some of those lightbulbs that use less electricity. "We've all got to do our bit," he said. "By the way, Lyall, I hope you switched that computer off while you're not using it."

"Sunny, I can't believe you burned *today's* paper," said Mum anxiously.

"You're looking a bit tense, love," said Carl, hugging the ladder with one arm and Mum with the other. "How 'bout I make us a vodka tonic?"

Mum looked as though she was about to burst. Her face was red, her brow was twisted up and her jaw jutted out. She'd dropped the girly act completely. At that moment, I have to say I actually missed it, because even though the girly act was fake, at least it wasn't scary.

"Carl, I *told* you," she said without moving her lips, "I can't have any alcohol until after I finish my hypnosis. I've told you three times. No alcohol, okay?"

"Sorry, love, totally forgot. I'll get us a mineral water instead." He filled two glasses and cut some fresh lemon. "Hey," he said. "Did you ever hear the one about the three men on a train? There was an Irishman, an American and—"

"Daaaaaad-duh!" shrieked Lyall and Saskia.

"Fine," said Carl. "Gee, it's really *joy to the world* over here tonight, isn't it?"

I was staring into the fire, trying not to cry about what Claud had said, or about Granny Carmelene, and glad for all the commotion to take the attention away. Maybe Claud was right and I am the sort of person who finds it hard to share. Maybe it's all part of being an only-child introvert.

Mum handed me the profit jar. "Sunny, you should really apologize to Claud. No one likes to be accused of something they didn't do."

"Sorry, Claud," I said, putting the jar back in the fridge.

"It helps if you look at someone when you apologize, Sunny," said Mum, "as though you really mean it."

I gave Mum *the eyebrow,* as if to say *You know, Mum, I think I preferred you as a smoker. You might die sooner, but at least you'd be a more chilled-out person.*

"Sorry, Claud," I said, darting her a look, and feeling a little embarrassed for getting the stealing part so wrong.

"Me too," said Claud. "Let's just forget about it and get on with our orders."

"Sounds like a good idea," said Carl, handing Mum her mineral water.

"So?" asked Lyall, wiping down a chopping board. "Is Buster going to come next week or what? Or is this just going to be a lifelong girlfest?"

"Can we just get on with making pizzas?" I asked.

"I guess a vote would be fair," said Carl. "Hands up, who's in favor!"

I don't need to tell you which way that one panned out!

 was sooo glad to be at Dad's on Saturday. Steph and I went shopping at Chadstone for itsy-bitsy singlets and baby suits for Flora to wear home from hospital. They were size 000 and didn't even look big enough for Boris. We had to get ones that weren't obviously girly, so as not to give away the secret about Flora to Dad.

"I think all this pink and blue stuff is silly anyway," said Steph. "Not to mention those ridiculous baby hair bands! Why does a baby have to advertise its gender?"

"Me too," I said, helping Steph with the shopping bags. She had a list from the hospital of all the things she needed to pack.

"Nighties!" said Steph as she crossed the baby suits off the list. "I can't remember the last time I even owned a nightie."

It made me think about Mum, and whether she had been as excited about me being born as Steph was about Flora, and whether she bought me tiny baby suits too. And how it was for Granny Carmelene being big and pregnant with Mum. And how it could happen that something makes that closeness end, and a gap gets in the way—like the gap I could feel growing between Mum and me. Maybe the gap gets wider because nobody does anything about stopping each other from drifting away, or about building a bridge.

When Steph and I got home, Dad was in his basketball-coaching gear.

"How're my two favorite girls?" he asked, beaming, and gave Steph and me a kiss. "Ready for the match today, Sunny? It'll be a tough one. I want to get down early so—"

"—so we can have a good warm-up session before the game," I finished for him. "Yes, Coach!" And I saluted him like they do in the army. I wanted to tell Dad and Steph about Tasmania. I really did. Mostly because I could feel the Stash-O-Matic reaching maximum capacity. But instead I made up a fresh new lie: I told them I was hanging with Ruby Carter in the morning, then staying at Mum's on Sunday night. Then I just had *one* more lie to tell Mum—that I'd be staying at Dad's on Sunday night, instead of her place.

Then my lying career would definitely be over. Promise! (If you can believe that.) I thought about inventing some sort of an electric shock device, just in case lying *did* become a habit. Something that would really hurt. Maybe the Tangent Police would be better at detecting lies than tangents.

Buster Conroy got two three-pointers in a row. Can you believe it? One of them was even a swish. It's hard to be unhappy with someone who's just helped your team win, even if he is a totally dodgy individual who took your friend away. Being so happy about the big win made me happier with Claud, too. Plus I wanted to prove to her that I could share. I even told Claud about having to lie my way to Tasmania, but not about You Know What. (Granny Carmelene's illness, I mean.) Letting it slip was tempting, but I didn't want to inflict such a heavy secret on Claud—even if a burden shared is a burden halved, as *They* say.

"So, Tassie tomorrow? What's she like, this long-lost grandmother, anyway? And when are you going to tell your mum? It's like you're having an affair, Sunny, with your granny!" said Claud, banging the locker door shut in the change rooms.

"Mum would kill me," I said. "Besides, all we ever talk about these days is who's going to do the dishes. Need a lift home, Claud? Dad's out in the car."

"It's okay, I'm catching the tram. Gotta fly. Thanks anyway, though." Claud grabbed her bag and ran out of the change room, calling over her shoulder, "I'll ring you tonight, Sunny, to say farewell!"

I looked at myself close-up in the mirror, and washed the sweat off my face. I stared deep into my own eyes and wondered if anyone else could see all the secrets behind them just from looking at me.

When I was in the car with Dad I saw Claud and Buster running across the football field to the tram stop. I think they were holding hands, but I couldn't be totally sure. Either way, seeing them running off like that was like watching a silent movie, in slow motion. It was sort of lovely. And because it was in slow motion, it gave me time to see clearly the things that sometimes happen too fast to notice. Like how life had made a gap between Claud and me, and how I had blamed the gap on Buster.

He was just someone who Claud had invited in, just like I was doing with Granny Carmelene.

At dinner I asked Dad and Steph if I could move in with them for a while as a backup plan.

"I could help with Fl—the baby too," I said to Steph, passing her the beans.

"Sunny," said Dad, "it's not that we don't want you here. You know we do. I'm more concerned about you wanting to give up on your home life with Mum, just because a few challenges have been thrown in. You can't always run away."

"Well, it doesn't feel like home anymore. Even Willow's being bossed about by a cat. It's just not dignified. Is there any dessert?"

"No," said Steph, "but only for a little while longer. As soon as this baby's born, I'm having a carbohydrate party." And she rubbed her belly as she laughed.

"Look, Sunny, you're going through some big changes all round. Give yourself some time to adjust. It'll all settle down, I promise you. Now you better get organized for tomorrow. If you're going to be with Ruby all day and you want to stay the night at Mum's, you'll need to pack all your things for school on Monday too."

NINETEEN

Granny Carmelene had a big old Mercedes with fins on either side at the back. It was a buttery cream color. She had the engine running and was cleaning the windows with scrunched-up newspaper when I walked down the drive.

"It needs a bit of time to warm up," Granny said. "Just like its owner." She gave me a kiss on the cheek. "I'm so excited, Sunny, and so happy you could come."

"Me too," I said, putting my overnight bag in the open trunk.

"Could you run inside for me?" She pointed toward the house. "I've made a fresh hummingbird cake and a thermos of tea. God knows if there'll be any decent tea on board the boat. Best to bring your own, I say. I've nearly finished these windows."

I passed the drawing room, and the ancestors' eyes made me feel instantly guilty again, so I glanced over my shoulder to make sure Granny Carmelene couldn't see me and then gave them the finger on my way to the kitchen. I really wanted to have a snoop upstairs, but it's bad manners to ask to look around someone's house. You should wait until they offer, or maybe just drop hints.

"Thank you, Sunday," said Granny Carmelene as I carried the basket outside. "You can put it in the trunk." She was wearing another color-coordinated outfit: a pleated cream linen skirt, a silky blouse with a peacock-feather design, which did up at the neck, and a matching jacket. There was a dark chocolate handbag on the front seat, which totally matched her shoes.

"Is there anything else, Granny, that I can do?" I was hoping she'd ask me to get something from her bedroom so that I could have a peek in her wardrobe. It must have been like a department store up there.

"Let me see, I think we're almost done. I'll just do a quick security check and lock the doors. You get in and choose some music. There're a whole lot of CDs in the glove box."

I looked through Granny Carmelene's CDs. I hadn't heard of most of them, but I could tell they must have been old style because there were names like Billie Holiday and Nina Simone. And there were

some French ones by someone calle
and also Serge Gainsbourg, who had
and smoked a cigar. I put the Édith Pia
player as Granny got in the driver's seat besi
We both looked at our watches. It was nearly s
o'clock.

"Do you know what this song means, Sunny?"

I was looking at the CD cover. "No, but I am going
to be learning French when I get to Year Seven. I can't
wait."

"She says '*Non, je ne regrette rien,*' I regret nothing.
They called her the Little Sparrow. She had a very difficult life, apparently, but no regrets."

I didn't really know what Granny Carmelene was
talking about, or what Édith Piaf was singing about,
for that matter. But I listened carefully to the song
anyway, and how the music built up and up and made
my body tingle, which meant absolutely and undeniably that it must have been about something important.

"You should never have regrets, Sunday; there is
only learning."

"Okay, I won't." I wished I'd chosen a different CD
because the whole topic was making my secret adventure feel heavy and serious when I wanted to feel
naughty and free—even if my traveling companion
did have a life-threatening condition and was about
a hundred.

Granny Carmelene had reserved a twin cabin on the *Spirit of Tasmania*'s deck eight. We parked the car

down below and made our way up the stairs and narrow walkways to our room. The cabin had two single beds on either side of a porthole window, and a very small bathroom. Granny unpacked the thermos of tea and the cake onto the bedside table, and hung her jacket up on the back of the door.

"Don't let me forget that, Sunny, will you?"

"I know, let's put the car keys in the pocket," I said. "That way if you forget your jacket we won't be able to start the car, which will make you remember to go and get your jacket."

"What a clever idea," said Granny Carmelene, putting her car keys in the pocket of her jacket and hurrying back to sit on the little bed, as if she might have fallen over if it wasn't there.

"You don't mind if I take a little rest, do you, Sunny? Did you bring something to read? Afterward, we'll go for cocktails."

"I'll be fine, Granny. I'd like to explore, anyway. Maybe look in the gift shop. Do you *feel* sick, with CLL, I mean? Does it hurt or anything?"

"Oh, I have my good days and my bad days, Sunny. It comes and goes. Sometimes for months and months I'm as right as rain, and then suddenly I can't get out of bed for days, which is why I have to seize the moment when I've got energy for adventures. I'm slowing down now, though. I can feel it, but it's a peaceful time, too, and right. I plan to slip away quietly, when my time comes. I can already sense how gentle it will be."

I went out an exit door to the back deck. We were already a long way from shore. I could just see the hazy outline of the city across the water. It reminded me of New York, even though I've never been there. I edged down to the back of the boat, holding the handrail all the way. The sea was calm, but I felt as if the wind might blow me off. It hurt my ears. There was a man in a bluey jacket sitting at a table having a Big M chocolate milk and trying to read a paper that was flapping in the wind.

"Getting a bit nippy," he said, folding his newspaper under his arm. "Might head back inside."

I held on to the cold white railing at the very back of the boat and leant over to where I could hear the engines roaring and see the water churning like a washing machine. It reminded me of the part in *Titanic* where Leonardo DiCaprio and Kate Winslet first kiss, but then I got off that topic entirely because it made me think about Claud and Buster and how sickening it would be if they actually were kissing. So instead I thought about the Stash-O-Matic and in particular about throwing it overboard. I could hear the crunching of metal as it got all munched up by the propellers. And then I had scary imaginings about leaning over too far and falling into the deep dark water and waving like crazy but nobody noticing that I'd gone, and having to watch the *Spirit of Tasmania* head off without me.

When I got back to our cabin there was a note from Granny Carmelene saying she would meet me at the lounge bar on deck seven for a cocktail before dinner.

When I found the bar, she was sitting at a table in a curvy blue chair that wrapped around her like a clamshell.

"There you are, Sunny. Isn't this lovely?" she said as a waiter delivered two drinks to our table. "The perfect remedy after a catnap! How was your exploring?"

"Great," I said. "I bought a postcard, even though I'll be home before I get to send it."

"I ordered a couple of martinis, although yours, I'm afraid, is a mock martini."

I didn't tell Granny Carmelene how I'd had a champagne once—at Claud's for her mum's fortieth—or how it made me wobble. I was feeling suddenly uneasy. What if Mum and Dad had spoken to each other and I'd been busted doing my disappearing act? What if they'd called Claud and cross-examined her?

I sat down on the other blue clamshell chair.

Granny Carmelene held up her glass. "Cheers, Sunday," she said as we clinked our martini glasses together. "Here's to building bridges and a lifetime of adventures."

"Cheers, Granny," I said, and then I just blurted out, "Whatever happened to Grandpa Henry?"

"Good lord, girl, you certainly know how to spoil a moment!" she said, clunking her glass back down on the table.

"Sorry, Granny, it's just that—"

"I know, Sunday, I know. You're just trying to piece things together. It must be very confusing."

"I just don't think all these wonderings are good for my imagination. It makes me think too much about all the possibilities. I'm scared my imagination is going to run out of ideas because I've wasted them all on trying to work out everybody else's secrets."

"You're absolutely right, dear." Granny Carmelene took another sip of her drink, and a deep breath. "Here goes, then. Your grandfather, although a charming character in many ways, was somewhat of a *ladies' man,* if you know what I mean. Quite unfaithful. Although I never knew the half of it."

I wasn't really sure what a *ladies' man* was. I thought maybe it meant dressing up—like the men in the Sydney Mardi Gras.

"Does that mean Grandpa Henry wore lipsti—"

"It means, in short, my girl, that one day Henry took off to live abroad with my very own sister—and I never saw either of them ever again. They'd been carrying on with one another for years, as it turned out, behind my back."

I felt a flash of cold down one side of my body, even though there was nowhere that the cold could have been getting in.

"Was Mum very old?"

"Old enough! Yes, Sunday, she knew all along and said absolutely nothing. It was quite clear where your mother's loyalty was. Not with me. Not with her own mother. And it's the same today, I can assure you."

"But maybe she—"

"My dear Sunday," Granny said, holding up her glass to toast again. "May you discover many things, but may you *never* know betrayal." Granny Carmelene's lips grew tight and thin, and for the first time I could see a resemblance to Mum.

"So it's not only that Mum isn't forgiving you, but also that you've never forgiven her?"

"Something like that," said Granny Carmelene, looking away. "Time doesn't always heal," she added under her breath.

"Why did you send Mum a present, then? At Christmas."

"Because years and years of *not* forgiving is exhausting, and I was hoping to get to you, Sunday. I did it for you."

It was pretty hard to get over that conversation, I can tell you. Granny Carmelene was all glassy-eyed and inward while we ate dinner, and I felt awful for forcing her to remember things that made her unhappy. I think it's what *They* call being a killjoy. Still, it was a dead relief to find out the reasons for the divorce. I could see how one divorce could cause another, and how not knowing the real truth could make you get all your opinions and feelings in a muddle. I felt  bad for being so angry with Mum. I mean, it wasn't exactly her fault that Grandpa Henry was a ladies' man. And it must have been awful to get the blame.

With all those bad feelings inside it's no wonder she's addicted to cigarettes. I wanted to go back to Mum's—to go home—right away, which wasn't such an easy thing to want, on account of being halfway across Bass Strait on a secret adventure. But it was good to feel like home was really home again—even if it did have a lot of new rules and a whiteboard.

TWENTY

I woke to the sound of Granny Carmelene zipping her bag. It felt very early. I knelt on my bed and peered out the porthole.

"We're less than an hour away, Sunny, just enough time for some breakfast." Granny Carmelene was already dressed. "Should I meet you down in the cafeteria?" she asked.

I wasn't that hungry, to be honest. I still had a tummy full of dinner, not to mention the humming-bird cake we'd had for supper in our cabin, before bed. But I agreed to meet her in the cafeteria because I was feeling super grateful. Not only had Granny Carmelene finally revealed the answer to the biggest mystery of my life, but she had also introduced me to an entirely forgotten food group: peas! Can you believe neither Mum *nor* Dad had ever given them to me before? Honestly, I think I should call the Kids Help Line. Peas are delicious and perfectly round and really fun to eat . . . but I know I'm on a tangent, so I'll get back to the story. And as if there is anyone reading this who has never tried a pea.

"Bring the map down with you, Sunny," said Granny Carmelene as she left the cabin, "so we're clear on exactly where we need to go. I'm thinking we skip the A1 and take the B13. The back roads always make a nicer journey."

Granny Carmelene took a pair of large round sunglasses and a pair of short leather driving gloves from the glove box. I liked the way she drove the car—sort of too slow, but in a good way that made turning corners last longer. I was more comfortable with her now, and I didn't have to feel bad about not knowing what to talk about, or worry about saying dumb things to stop myself from blurting out things that I shouldn't mention. Finding out the *answer* to a mystery was just as relieving as getting rid of a secret. It's as though no matter which side of a secret you are on, that secret's got a hook through you, and it's pulling you about like a fish caught on a line.

I checked the map and directed us out of Devonport and onto the B13. The sun was gentle through the glass. I closed my eyes and felt it warm my face for a few moments, and I wanted to go back to sleep. But I was the navigator, so I pulled my attention back to the map so as not to miss the turnoff for Mole Creek. I thought about school and how I was meant to be there and how far away I was from being anywhere at all.

Granny Carmelene eased the car into a parking lot at King Solomon Cave. We were the only ones there, I guess because it was a Monday and most people do cave visits on weekends.

"With any luck we'll have a private tour," said Granny Carmelene as she locked the car. "What a godsend!"

We bought two tickets for the next tour from Perry, the tour guide. Apparently no one is allowed to go into the caves alone. You might be tempted to graffiti them, I suppose. I'd never met anyone called Perry before, which made me think it could be a Tasmanian name in particular. It happens like that, you know.

We were a little early, which is common for on-time people, kind of like getting to see the sun rise while everyone else was still asleep.

Perry told us some facts about the caves before we went inside: how they were discovered (the farmer in the twenties, chasing the wallaby); how they were nine meters below the surface (gulp!); and how we'd be going through a series of natural chambers full of stalactites and stalagmites, which were formed over millions and millions of years from water droplets seeping through rock crystals and minerals back when Australia was part of Gondwana. Then he took us down a narrow sloping path toward the opening, and Granny Carmelene clutched my hand.

The first thing I noticed was the temperature dropping. Maybe we'll all be living in caves when global warming goes nuts? Maybe Osama bin Laden is on to something with all that cave-hiding, although, come to think of it, he's probably all holed up in a Gucci cave with gold-leaf stalactites. I wondered if I should change my school design project to a cave. Granny Carmelene must have read my mind.

"Is this not the greatest work of art, Sunny?" she said as we made our way between two enormous stalactite columns. They were wet and glistening, as if alive. I touched one and it was cold, which made it seem dead and alive all at the same time. I looked up to the ceiling, which was one of the highest I've ever seen and not at all what I was expecting from a cave.

"Of all our earthly endeavors, Sunny, all the great works of architects and engineers, and artists—to think that *this* has been here all along. Just think, some of our most respected minds have merely been reproducing nature without even knowing it."

"Gosh," I said, thinking that maybe I had *inherited* the tangent thing from Granny Carmelene. Just like I've obviously inherited a gene for divorce.

"When God wants you to do something, Sunday, you *think* it's your own idea."

It felt like being inside the stomach of an enormous slumbering beast, but one that smelled like rock. The walls were pinkish, which Perry said was because of the iron in the rock. In some places the color turned more yellow, which was apparently due to calcium. There were stalactites and stalagmites everywhere, which sometimes looked as though they were dripping from the ceiling, and in other places as though they were melting out of the walls. Some had even joined together to form pillars of curtained rock that you could squeeze through, like a doorway.

We went deeper and deeper into the earth, and each chamber was slightly different, and slightly colder than the last. Perry showed us the original entrance in the ceiling where the wallaby had fallen in, and I wondered if the wallaby had ever got out again and hoped it hadn't broken anything in the fall.

Granny Carmelene squeezed my hand. "Isn't it marvelous, Sunny?"

"I've never seen anything like it," I said. "It's like being inside a lung."

"Or inside the womb of the great mother," she murmured.

"Or a cathedral," I whispered as we squeezed through an opening into the last chamber.

"Ah, yes," she said. "This is the place." And she took a deep breath and held it in.

Perry must have sensed something, because he stopped talking about the caves and said he'd give us time to be alone. The rock formations were like the pipes of the biggest organ I'd ever seen, and a shaft of light shone through a crack in the ceiling.

Granny Carmelene became very quiet and very still, and leant into me, not letting go of my hand. I wasn't sure what to do, or what there *was* to do, other than to sort of prop her up and sway back at her with the same amount of sway she had toward me.

She started humming as we swayed. Then the hum turned into a type of singing, as though her voice was a crystal-clear musical instrument. The sound bounced all over the cave walls and back at me, making my body shiver. I felt warm, then suddenly cold, as though I was stretching out of my body, then shrinking back in again.

Granny Carmelene's voice was like nothing I'd ever heard before. And all the echoes made it sound like a whole choir, which reminded me of harps and lyres and angels. I know you probably won't believe this, but I really did see an angel,

disappearing up and fading into the shaft of light.
I really did.

That night on the *Spirit of Tasmania* I wrote a postcard
to my little baby nearly born sister, Flora.

Dear Flora, ♡
I'm on my way home,
and so are you.
I'll see you soon.
Love, Sunny xx

Flora Hathaway♡
Dad's house
Melbourne
Australia
The World

AFFIX STAMP HERE

Willow jumped and leapt and spun all around me when I came home from school on Tuesday. I could hardly get in the front gate. She raced up and down the driveway and did laps while I was getting the spare key out from its hiding place under the brick near the shed. Boris was watching from up on the garden wall, hissing as Willow sped past.

"Come on, girl," I said. "Let's have ourselves a bit of couch time while no one's home."

There was a note from Mum on the kitchen table.

Dear Sunny,
    Looks like it's just you and
        me tonight.

Feel like chicken in Pajamas —
at the RSL?
I'll be home 6ish
Love Mum x
P.S. I missed you!

I kicked off my shoes and lay back on the couch. I had so many big feelings churning around all at once, and I wasn't sure which one to pay the most attention to. I was happy for Granny Carmelene that she got to go to King Solomon Cave, but sad because it had felt like she was saying goodbye. I mean, what else could it have been, given that there was an angel? And I felt guilty about Mum, and how I'd done so much behind her back—and for how I had thought she was so cold-hearted. I felt relieved to be home alone, just like the good old days, and better about Claud and me, and excited about Flora, who was coming really soon. It was all too much.

I closed my eyes and imagined myself up to seat 44K, but I was plonked back on the couch again because both 44K and 44J were occupied by loud Americans, and the rest of the flight was completely full. So I turned the TV on, which is the next best thing when you really need to avoid your feelings.

Mum and I walked down to the back-room restaurant at the Elwood RSL. I actually liked it far better before the grumpy new owners took all the giant wooden salad servers off the wall and painted everything beige and hung a boring picture. I mean, salad bowls on the wall are far more interesting, but maybe that's just me wanting everything to stay the same, no matter how much Mum keeps saying: *The only thing that never changes, is that everything changes.* Boy, am I tired of hearing *that* one.

We ordered our dinners and sat down. I really wanted to tell Mum about the *Spirit of Tasmania,* but I couldn't, which is *another* reason why secrets are totally bad news. Mum would have loved to hear about the cabins and the tiny little windows, not to mention the caves.

"Did you hear any news on Buster's mum, Sunny?"

"They still haven't found her," I said. "They think she may be sailing to Vanuatu with some guy she met who needed a cook on his boat. That's what her last boss said anyway, the one on Great Keppel Island."

"You'd think she'd at least *write,*" Mum said, sipping her red wine.

"Yeah, she's not being exactly *motherly,*" I said, and then I remembered how Granny Carmelene hadn't been exactly *motherly* either, and I felt bad again, for both of them.

Mum must have read my mind, because right after the waiter brought our meals to the table, she looked me right in the eye and said, "Sunny, you haven't contacted your grandmother, have you? You haven't broken your promise?"

So that I didn't have to tell a lie, I said, "Would you care if she died, Mum?" and focused very hard on cutting my chicken.

"I'd care, Sunny. I'd hope she died in peace. I'd hope she didn't suffer. I'd hope her life was fulfilled. I don't wish her any harm, but that doesn't mean we have a relationship, not one that works. It's not going to change anything when she dies. Dying has nothing to do with it, Sunny."

"Do you want some pepper?" I asked, passing over the grinder.

"Sunny—you didn't answer my question."

It wasn't only because I could still hear the faint and gurgled pinging of the Stash-O-Matic all the way at the bottom of the sea that I ended up telling Mum the truth. It was mostly because my head felt so *cluttered*, and I was in the habit of having Mum help me get my cluttered feelings in order. Besides, I really wanted to hear her side of the story about Granny Carmelene and Grandpa Henry (because there *are* always two sides to a story, sometimes even more). I told her everything—even about wagging school and even about going to Tasmania, which meant she'd tell on me to Dad and Steph and I'd get in trouble for lying to them, too. The only thing I didn't tell was about

Granny Carmelene's *condition,* because that was a secret that I still felt was important to keep, and not one that involved lying to anybody or sneaking about.

Mum was *really* angry about the Tasmania part.

"For God's sake, Sunny, what if the damn boat had sunk?" She called the waiter over and asked for another glass of red wine.

But I hardly noticed the trouble I was in at all, and hardly listened to a thing Mum said. Besides, I wasn't necessarily sorry about what I'd done, just about the order I'd done it in. Finally Mum stopped talking and gave a deep sigh.

"I just wanted to help you and Granny make up," I said. "I really thought I could."

"I know, love. I know you were trying to figure things out," said Mum, reaching over to hold my hand.

"And you just wouldn't give me any answers, and—"

"It's painful for me, Sunny, to be blamed all these years for something I shouldn't have even had to know about. If I'd told my mother what I knew, it would have caused more trouble than I thought I could handle, and I really wanted to believe it wasn't happening, so I just ignored it and hoped it wasn't real. I convinced myself it wasn't true—not to mention how angry I was with my father *and* Aunt Clementine."

"Granny's own sister! And I just thought having a brother would be bad."

"It's what you call a double betrayal, Sunny. It's the worst sort."

All that trouble had made me lose my appetite, so I drew my knife and fork together and Mum did too, even though she'd hardly touched her meal either. "I hope the chef doesn't take it personally." She smiled.

"Mum, I *like* Granny Carmelene. I don't like how she was with you, but I *like* how she is with me."

"It's all right, Sunny," Mum said. "I understand. I used to like her too, you know." And she looked hard up to the ceiling and tipped her head back a little, to try to make her tears go back in.

Before I went to bed I snuck outside with the cordless phone and rang Granny Carmelene. I was worried about her coming back from Tasmania to an empty house, even though I'm sure for her it was nothing new.

"I'm perfectly fine, thank you, Sunday. I feel remarkably refreshed, actually, and came home to the most wonderful news from my art dealer. Would you believe, he's managed to locate one of the most precious maps on earth, an original, one of the old Chinese ones I told you about, from the fourteen hundreds?"

"That's amazing," I said.

"It is indeed. I can't wait for you to see it, Sunday. It's made me sing with joy all day!"

TWENTY-TWO

Dad was dead angry when Mum told him about my secret trip to Tasmania, especially as Steph was about to have the baby. That's the trouble with divorced parents who are still friendly: you can't get away with half the stuff that kids do who have the sort of divorced parents who swap them over in the play-ground on Wednesday afternoons and only speak about whose turn it is to pay for things. Mum and Dad spent ages on the phone thinking up a suitable pun-ishment. I was just hoping Mum didn't talk it over with Carl, because he'd come up with a beauty, for sure. Can you imagine? It would be dishes duty for the rest of my life. You'd think Mum and Dad would at least have some compassion, though. I mean, I couldn't tell them about Granny Carmelene's illness, but I did at least own up to my crime. Surely that should lighten my sentence?

Meanwhile, Boris had taken over Willow's dog bed. Every time Willow snuck past, Boris stood up and growled, swiping at Willow with a front paw. Boris also ate Willow's dinner. Willow just sat like the Sphinx, but with her head on the floor, and waited until he had finished. Because Willow had nowhere to sleep at night, she'd taken to sneaking onto the bottom bunk in my room. Nobody had noticed, so I let her keep doing it. Besides, I was worried about Willow becoming depressed. I told Buster about it when we were practicing goals before school. He knew all about dogs, which not only made him far more interesting than I'd given him credit for and possibly even nice (don't tell!) but also made me think he might know some sort of way to help, or at least cheer Willow up.

"Cats always win in the end," he said. "But I'll think of something."

"Buster's going to give us a hand with Pizza-A-Go-Girl tonight," said Claud. "He's even got some new pizza ideas. Haven't you, Buster?" Claud nudged him with her elbow and gave him *the eyebrow*.

"Yep, might be just what you need." He smiled, then shot his second swish in a row. Buster's idea of *just what I need* was a bit of a worry. Especially when

Claud told me she'd caught Buster pashing the mirror when she accidentally walked in on him in the bathroom. Can you imagine? Whether he was pashing the mirror 'cos he loved himself, or whether he was practicing so that he could pounce on Claud, pashing a mirror is just about as wrong-town as you can get! Even Claud thinks so.

You'll never believe what Buster's idea was for Pizza-A-Go-Girl? Wait for it. . . . *Doggie pizzas!*

"Yeah, out of the scraps!" said Buster as he shaped some pizza dough into the shape of a bone. We all laughed.

"Dogs are big business, you know—and I was even thinking we could make our own cooking show, 'cos I've got Uncle Quinny's camera. Then when Mum gets back she won't feel like she's missed out on anything—that's if she ever does come back. . . ."

"Of *course* she will," said Claud as we all nodded.

"But maybe it was all my fault that she went?"

"Naaaah," I said, leaning against my pizza shovel, "she was obviously just well overdue for an adventure. She'll be back, I can feel it in my intuition."

Buster made doggie pizzas all night, including one for Willow in the shape of a cat, which he thought would help because it was psychological. Lyall did the deliveries, and Claud and Saskia and I finished up in the kitchen. I liked the dog pizza idea. I really did. It was cute. I just couldn't see how it made much business sense, which is an important consideration when you're an entrepreneur.

"Boy! That was the busiest night yet," said Saskia, taking off her apron.

"Yep," I said, counting the last of the money. "We made a hundred and fifty dollars. That's a record. Thanks, guys!"

Claud wrote everything down, because we're meticulous about book work and keeping records.

"When do we get to actually spend the money?" said Lyall. "What's the point of just keeping it in a jar?" I noticed he was pouring juice out of the bottle marked *Saskia*. That's how it is with brothers.

"Soon," said Claud. "But we've got to cover our overheads. We'll divide it all up at the end of June. That's when businesses work out their profits and have to pay tax."

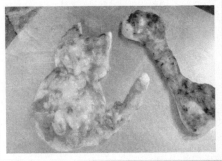

Mum came out to the shed with Willow racing along beside her. That Boris-shaped doggie pizza Buster made for her must have really worked, because she was looking like her old bouncy self again. Or maybe it was whatever he whispered in her ear, 'cos dogs understand stuff and maybe I hadn't been communicating properly.

"That was your dad on the phone, Sunny," Mum said excitedly. "Steph's gone into labor and they're on their way to the hospital!"

TWENTY-THREE

t was absolutely and undeniably impossible to sleep knowing that Steph was in the middle of having a baby. I kept waking up all night. Maybe she'd already had Flora, but Dad thought it was too early to call. Or maybe there were problems with the birth. Even Willow tossed and turned on the bottom bunk, making groany noises.

I had just got to sleep when I was woken by the sound of the phone. I knew straightaway it would be Dad, so I leapt out of bed.

"That's just wonderful, James," said Mum, and mouthed to me *It's a girl* as Carl came in with the Saturday papers.

I grabbed the phone. "Hey, Dad! Can I come down

now? Is Steph okay? Mum said she'd drive me! Can I come? Can I come?"

It seemed to take forever getting to the hospital. We were stuck in traffic nearly all the way down Punt Road and there wasn't even a big game on. Unfortunately, it gave Mum loads of nagging time.

"I want you to promise me that you'll never lie to us again," Mum said.

"I promise." This time I didn't have my fingers crossed.

Then she told me about all the extra jobs I had to do, which was when it became *totally* obvious that she *had* talked it over with Carl after all. It was one of those moments where you really wish cars could fly. Maybe ours could be fueled by some of the regret I felt about making such a mess of things, as well as some of the relief I felt at no longer having to keep in the secret that Dad and Steph's baby was a girl.

"Don't stay too long," Mum said as she dropped me off and gave me a kiss. "They've probably been up all night, and Steph will need to rest."

"Okay, I'll call you later. Thanks for the lift, Mum," I said, slamming the door.

"And don't slam the door!" Mum called out, just a little bit late.

Steph was propped up in bed surrounded by big white pillows. I'd never seen anyone look so happy and so tired all at the same time, like she'd just won a marathon at the Olympics. Dad was asleep in an armchair next to the bed. I tippee-toed in, being careful not to wake him, or Flora, who was bundled up and fast asleep in Steph's arms.

"Look, Sunny, she's perfect," whispered Steph. "Come and see."

Flora had the tiniest littlest hands, and her lips were perfectly rosebuddy red. I could tell you all sorts of cute and gorgeous things about Flora, but the thing that stuck out the most—which isn't really that cute and gorgeous—was that Flora had worry lines. Already! I mean, what is there to worry about floating around in someone's tummy when you're not even born yet? Maybe it meant that Flora was going to be an introvert, like me. She had three little worry lines across her forehead and a frown line right between her eyes. It was going to take her years to learn to talk, and to be able to tell me what she was so worried about. Maybe it was the lack of sugar.

"Sit down, Sunny," said Steph, patting the bed next to her. "You can hold her if you like." Steph wriggled over and I sat down.

"There you go, Flora," whispered Steph as she passed the little bundled Flora gently over to me. "It's your very own big sister, Sunny."

Flora hardly weighed anything, and I suddenly felt frightened that I might drop her, or that she might fall out from the bottom of the blanket, because I heard of that happening once and the baby got brain damage.

"She's the cutest," I said, edging further onto the bed. And Flora did the tiniest baby sneeze, which was seriously the sweetest thing I'd ever heard.

Dad's phone went off, but luckily it just vibrated silently in his pocket so it didn't give Flora a fright.

"It's your mother," he said, waking up and looking at his caller ID.

"Hi, Alex," he said croakily. "Thanks—yes, we're all still here—Sunny's having a cuddle now—Yes, thanks—Yes, it was a long night—She did really well—Seven pounds four—A little bit, she's got the same dark hair as Sunny—No, quiet as a mouse—Really? Oh, that's terrible. How did you hear?—Will *I* tell her?—Are *you* okay?—Was it a sudden thing, or—Okay, okay, bye."

I couldn't even say congratulations to Dad because I could tell by the look on his face that he had something important to say.

"Bad news, I'm afraid, Sunny. I'll come straight out with it—it's Granny Carmelene. She died in her sleep last night."

an you believe it? My baby sister got born and my grandmother died all in the middle of the same night! It was as if the news about Granny Carmelene thunderstruck all my feelings away. I just didn't think it would happen that soon. Sometimes knowing something is going to happen doesn't make it any less of a shock when it actually comes around.

Dad gave me a lift back to Mum's, and in the car I told him about Granny's CLL.

"Must have been quite a weight on your shoulders, Sunny, keeping that all to yourself."

"Guess so. Seems weird now, though." It wasn't that

I even felt sad, maybe because I knew Granny Carmelene felt so comfortable with the idea of dying and maybe because Flora arriving just made *sad* impossible.

"Did you know I've known that Flora was a girl ever since the ultrasound?" I said.

"Crikey, you kept that one quiet," said Dad. "I had no idea."

But even though Granny Carmelene made dying feel like just another part of life, and I knew she wasn't afraid, it's still weird for the people who are left behind to have someone just *disappear*.

The *only* positive part about life making enormous things happen all at once was that Dad completely forgot about nagging and making me promise to be a better person. I guess having a brand-new perfect daughter made the older, slightly dodgy one seem not so bad.

When I got home, Mum and Carl were in the shed making a cup of tea. I was nervous about how Mum might be reacting to the news about Granny Carmelene.

"Hi, guys," I said.

Mum came over and gave me a hug.

"Hi, darling," she said. "How are you feeling?"

I shrugged. I didn't really know how I was feeling. "I knew she was dying, Mum," I whispered. And then my emotions came flooding over me. I suddenly realized how important Granny Carmelene had become and how I would never see her again. Willow burst into the shed, chased by Boris, and buried her nose in between my knees.

"Oh, Willow, it's all right," I said tearily, patting her head. Boris took off outside and jumped up onto the fence, and Willow bolted out after him, trying to make out that she was in charge. That's how it is these days—Willow is the boss outside, and Boris is the boss inside.

If you didn't know someone had just been born and someone else had just died, you would swear it was just another ordinary day.

"She left a letter for you, apparently," Mum said. "It was found by the gardener, who was the one who discovered she had died and called me. She'd left our number by her bed. She must have known."

"Yeah, but I still didn't think when I kissed her goodbye after Tassie that it was actually *goodbye*."

"Cup of tea, Sunny?" asked Carl. "Biscuit?"

"No thanks," I said. "Where're Lyall and Saskia?" I was trying to change the topic. Just then, Carl's phone rang.

"That'll be them now," he said, taking the call outside.

Mum was looking all bent out of shape. She was flicking through the newspaper, but I could tell she wasn't actually reading it. Then she rummaged through her bag and handed me a photograph. It was an old black-and-white one in a silver frame that hadn't been polished for a while. It was a photo of Mum and Granny Carmelene when Mum was young, maybe just a bit older than me. They were outside Granny's big white and black house. Mum was leaning back into Granny Carmelene, who looked all glam like a movie star and had both arms around Mum, squeezing her from behind. Mum was smiling and looking like she was trying not to laugh, as if maybe Granny Carmelene was tickling her, or had just said something cheeky.

"You both look so happy," I said.

"We were," said Mum, "in that moment."

It made me feel sad again for Mum, because that photo was solid evidence that the broken-down thing between her and Granny Carmelene hadn't always been that way. It made me wonder what Mum did with all the happy bits. Maybe she just butted them out in the garden while no one was looking, like a cigarette she wasn't meant to be smoking.

I felt as though if I stared at the photograph for long enough I might make it come to life, or maybe Mum could be pulled inside it, and she and Granny Carmelene could start again from that day forward, and could change the ending. Mum came and stood behind me, holding me the way Granny had held her in the photo.

"You keep it, Sunny," she said, kissing the side of my cheek. "So you know how I've always remembered her, underneath it all." Then she started crying. I turned around and gave her a hug, noticing Carl and Willow hovering in the doorway, then both quickly turning away toward the garden.

"Don't cry, Mum. You'll make *me* cry," I sobbed.

"You don't understand, Sunny," Mum said, weeping. "It's not because I've lost her *now*, it's for the constant loss of what *could have* been."

 n the morning of Granny Carmelene's funeral, Mum gave me the envelope from Granny. I could feel something heavy inside, and when I opened it there was a letter and a key.

My dearest Sunday,

I feel these are my final words.

It is a wonderful evening, this night, at the edge of this life. I'm certain there will be others.

Thank you for the lovely gift you were to an old lady who has so much—but also not enough—of the important things, like time and granddaughters. Take this key to my safety-deposit box. I have left instructions with your father to show you the way. There is something there for you, which I'd like you to keep safe for me.

I am tired now, Sunday, so very tired. I can hear the sweetest music—that last song I sang, while you held my hand, is beckoning, like a siren.

I am not afraid. Tell your mother I'm so very sorry.

All my love to you, Sunday, until we meet again,

Your Grandmother,
Carmelene Aberdeen

xox

"Can't you come to the funeral with me?" I said to Mum as I put the letter back in its envelope, trying not to cry. "Can't you change your mind?"

"I can't, sweetheart, I just can't do it. I'm sorry." Her bottom lip went all wobbly, making me wish I could make it stop, like if I had the sort of mind that could remember jokes.

But I didn't have to go to the funeral alone—even though Dad couldn't come either because it was right at the same time Steph and Flora were coming home from hospital. Claud offered to come, and then Buster asked if he could too, 'cos not only would he get to miss a day of school, but he could also wear the suit that he'd bought from the thrift shop (and I guess he also didn't want to be alone 'cos he'd been feeling extra bad about his mum). Claud said that her brother, Walter, said that Buster had been crying in his sleep, and grinding his teeth. I was trying to practice having compassion, so I told Buster he could come.

Buster looked like a million bucks in his suit, almost handsome, even—but don't tell anyone I said that 'cos it doesn't mean anything. I think chimps are handsome too, remember?

I was worried that I'd cry too much at the funeral. I would have to do the crying for all of us, Mum and Granny Carmelene included. What if once I started I just couldn't stop? They'd have to take me away on a stretcher, and I'd get jabbed with huge needles while I tried to kick and scream the doctors away.

But as it turned out, Buster cried so much it made me *not* cry at all. Like he'd taken all the available tears for himself, which, if you ask me, is a totally typical boy thing to do. I mean, he didn't even *know* Granny Carmelene.

There was a coffin at the front of the church, and I wondered if Granny Carmelene was actually in it, or whether it was just for show. I kind of wanted to look inside, just to see what people wear when they're dressed up for their own funeral. I mean, who chooses that?

There were a lot of people in the church, and more arrived after the priest started speaking as though he and Granny Carmelene had been best friends.

"Carmelene Aberdeen was a remarkable woman. A woman of intelligence, dignity and enviable grace, who lived every moment as though it was her last."

I was swept off on a tangent when I heard the word *intelligence*. It reminded me that I always find it hard to remember if it has one *l* or two. Can you actually be intelligent if you can't spell the word *intelligent*? I mean, I know I'm intelligent (not a super brainiac) but I can't always spell *inteligent*. So does that mean I'm actually not intelligent at all? Buster nudged me with his elbow.

"Is that true?" he whispered.

"Is what true?" I realized I'd missed a whole chunk of what the priest said on account of being lost in my own thoughts, which was bad because it's not every day you go to your grandmother's funeral, and you'd think I'd have been able to stick with reality for an hour or so. I spent the rest of the service with my thumbnail just slightly digging into my finger, so that the discomfort would help me stay with the program.

Afterward, Claud and Buster and I stood around outside the church until Claud took off to find a loo. I was hoping there'd be sandwiches. I didn't know one person and felt all awkward because maybe some of them knew about *me*. Right when I was thinking that, a woman came over to where we were standing.

"You must be Sunday?" she said, holding out her hand. "I'm Marjorie Featherston. Your grandmother told me so much about you. So lovely you could get to know each other the way you did."

I shook Marjorie's hand. She had a thick mask of makeup, and earrings like chandeliers that looked like they would hurt, for sure, or maybe even light up.

"Hello," I said, not knowing what to say next, and noticing Marjorie was looking quizzically at Buster, who was still sniveling.

"And you must be . . . ?" She held her hand out to Buster.

"Buster Conroy," he said. "Yeah, me and Carmelgreen, we were, like, old mates," he said. "Like this." And he held up two fingers twisted around one another.

"Really?" said Marjorie, looking to me for validation. "How odd, she never said a thing—but that was our Carmelene, always the one to have a little something up her sleeve."

"Yep," I said, nodding and trying to nudge Buster without Marjorie seeing me. Sometimes a nudge is the next-best thing if you can't do *the eyebrow*.

"Well, lovely to meet you both. Are you coming to the burial?" I looked over to Buster, whose eyes had flooded with fresh tears simply at the mention of a burial.

"No," I said, "I said my goodbyes in Tasmania."

"Good for you! Very well, then, look after yourselves," Marjorie said, looking at Buster in a worried sort of way, before walking off.

"Sorry," said Buster, "I don't want to stop you going to your granny's burial."

"Nah, it's true what I said. Besides, the whole being buried thing really freaks me out. I don't want to remember her that way. I want to remember her singing with the angels in King Solomon Cave."

"Yeah," said Buster, wiping his eyes. "I have one of them memories of my mum. It was one hot summer night and we were down at the beach, eating fish 'n' chips off the hood of Dad's car, and they was all happy and loved each other and Mum  looked all pretty—sitting on the hood of Dad's car like she was on one of those Chiko Roll ads. That's what I remember," said Buster, with his eyes all welling up again, "when I think of Mum."

"Come on," I said, putting my arm around him. "Let's find Claud and get out of here."

Claud and Buster and I caught a train back to the city, and then a tram down to St. Kilda beach. We did cannon balls off the pier in our undies all afternoon, even though you're not meant to, because there was no one to tell us off.

veryone was in the shed kitchen when the three of us got back to my place. Mum, Carl, Lyall, Saskia, Willow *and* Boris. It was kind of nice to have them all there like a family—especially since it was the sort of family that had lit the whole shed with candles and jumped out from behind furniture when we came in, like a party.

"Surprise!" they all shouted at once.

"We've made a special feast!" chirped Saskia, beaming. "To cheer you up!"

"Wow!" I said, sensing all the trouble they'd gone to. The shed had never looked so lovely and felt magical with all the candles lit. They had even made punch. I gave Mum a big hug.

"How'd you go?" she whispered in my ear.

"We're having dessert first up," interrupted Lyall. "Hey, like your suit, Buster."

"Yeah, suave," agreed Carl with a smile.

"What do you mean dessert first up?" I asked.

"Well," said Carl, "there's absolutely no reason why you can't have dessert first and the main course later, so, because tonight is such a special night, we're having dessert first. And not just *any* dessert either."

"Guess!" squealed Saskia, jumping up and down.

"Frog in a pond?" I asked. They all shook their heads.

"Pavlova?"

"Nah," said Lyall.

"Custard?" asked Buster. "I love custard."

"Can I tell? Can I tell?" shrieked Saskia.

"Wait, Saskia, surely they can do better than that," said Mum, cheekily.

"Chocolate mousse! I love chocolate mousse too!" said Buster.

"It's *so* not chocolate mousse," laughed Lyall. "Actually, there's a surprise for you, too, Buster, but Sunny's surprise is—"

"It's baked Alaska, Sunny! Baked alaska. Your favorite!" Saskia blurted out, clapping her hands.

"No!" I searched the shed with my eyes for some evidence. "Where?"

Carl was getting something out of the oven—not the wood oven, but the one connected to the stove. It was baked Alaska, all right. Just how it looked in the book. Like a mountain of snowy meringue that was crispy from the oven.

"And now," said Carl, "for the most spectacular part!" He poured some liqueur over the top and lit a match, making the whole thing come alive with blue and yellow flames that licked around the sides. "Flaming baked Alaska! Grab some plates and cutlery, Lyall!"

"Wait!" said Mum. "We want to give Buster his surprise before it stops flaming!"

Buster was looking nervously around the room as if to say *What on earth could beat that?*

"Who will do the drumroll?" said Carl. "Claud? One drumroll, please!"

Claud beat her hands on the edge of the table and Lyall and Saskia joined in. I was still transfixed by the baked Alaska and also a bit nervous, in an excited way, about what they could possibly be up to.

And then a woman stepped into the shed. She had blond hair that looked like it might be another color underneath, and she wore the tightest jeans I'd ever seen on a grown-up. Buster went as pale as a sheet.

"Mum!" he said, gently, as though he'd lost his loud voice completely.

Buster's mum held out her arms. "Come here, you! Got a hug for your old mum? Look at you, all dressed up, too!"

* * *

Well, if I didn't cry at Granny Carmelene's funeral, I sure did cry when Buster got his mum back. Even Claud cried, and that's saying something. It turned out Buster's mum had had no idea about Quinny going to jail. And it had taken ages to track her down because she had been working on a boat, and not the type of boat with a phone or e-mail. And even though I'd been sort of angry with Buster's mum for nicking off, I didn't want to spoil a baked Alaska occasion with negative emotions. Let's face it, it doesn't happen every day, and did I mention it was worth waiting nearly twelve years for?

Besides, I was tired of trying to work out why things were the way they were. I just thought about how we were having Buster and his mum for a back-to-front dinner and that nothing else mattered. That's what Granny Carmelene would have done.

TWENTY-SEVEN

A couple of days later, Dad took me into the bank where Granny Carmelene had her safety-deposit box. It was a big one in the city, with circular moving doors and lots of marble. Dad had made an appointment with one of the banker people so we didn't have to stand in line, and got to sit down at a special desk—I guess for people who have a special key, like I had.

"Miss Hathaway, we've been expecting you," said the banker man as I handed him the key. "Please, have a seat," he said, pointing to the chairs behind his desk. Dad and I both sat down.

"Firstly," he went on, "I'm very sorry to hear about your grandmother's passing. We've been looking after her for over forty years. Marvelous woman."

"Yes," I said, beginning to become unbearably curious about what it was that Granny wanted me to keep for her. I watched the man walk away and thought how Buster would really like his suit. Dad and I didn't say much. I think he was exhausted from being woken up all night by Flora. That's normal for babies, apparently. *So* not normal for Dad, though; not since I was a baby, anyway.

Soon enough the banker man returned carrying a large flat folio, like the ones artists have, or architects. Maybe Granny had given me one of the portraits of the ancestors, which would be good and all, but not really something I'd want to hang in my room, if you know what I mean.

"Now, Miss Hathaway. I have to say you are a *very* fortunate young lady." He put the folder down on the desk in front of us and opened it up. There was a layer of tissue paper, which he swept to one side, and under that was a map, one of Granny's maps.

"Of course!" I said. "I forgot about the maps."

"Not just *any* map, Miss Hathaway. This one is *most* rare. An original Chinese map dating back to the early fourteen-twenties. Only a couple of them have been found in the world."

"Oh—*that* map! I know the one. Granny

Carmelene had only just found it. It was her absolute prize possession." I was completely overwhelmed, not just that Granny had chosen me to have something so valuable to her, but also because I didn't really know what to *do* with the map. I mean, it was ten million times better than getting one of the ancestor portraits, but still, what's a girl to do with a map like that?

"Gee, Sunny," said Dad. "This thing's probably worth an absolute fortune."

"We have a valuation certificate and a certificate of authenticity right here," said the banker man, looking over his glasses. "Miss Hathaway has inherited something that is not only of incredible cultural significance, but is also a fairly substantial asset for a young lady." He slid a document over to Dad.

"Crikey, Sunny!" He pushed the certificate over toward me. I know you're probably really wanting to know how much that map was worth, but I'm not going to tell you, because in the end it makes no difference. I'm never, ever going to sell it. Granny Carmelene had asked me to keep the map, and that was exactly what I was going to do. It was her dying wish, after all. Besides, it's undignified to tell people how much things cost. Granny Carmelene said so herself. Boy, were there a lot of zeros, though!

"We suggest you leave the map here, safely locked away, until you're a little older. How does that sound, Miss Hathaway?"

"Perfect!" I said, feeling very relieved that I didn't have to be responsible for it or for someone ruining it by accident, now that I had so many siblings.

"You can access it any time you like," said the banker man. "Just give me a call and I'll arrange it for you." He gave me his personal business card, and I put it in the envelope that Granny Carmelene had left, with the letter and the key.

On the way back to Dad's I thought about making business cards for Pizza-A-Go-Girl, but then realized that pizza making wasn't the only thing I wanted to do, being an entrepreneur and all. Maybe I could have a business card saying *Sunny Hathaway, Harebrained schemes that usually work,* which would possibly cover everything that I'm interested in for the rest of my life.

Flora spent all her time nursing or sleeping. It's what babies do. Steph's breasts had grown to scarily giant proportions on account of all the milk they had inside them, and Steph had stopped wearing normal clothes. She just got about in tracksuit pants and a huge bra, which opened up at the front so that Flora could feed. Sometimes Steph would walk around with her bra all opened up and I didn't know where to look. I was worried that it had become so normal for her that she'd forget one day and go to the shops with

MARION ROBERTS was born in Melbourne, Australia, where she still lives today. When she was young, she loved to sew and make her own clothes, so believed she was destined to become a fashion designer. Instead, she found herself studying science, alternative medicine, and psychotherapy, which wasn't such a helpful combination for a job in the fashion industry. She worked as a naturopath and counselor, and because she also knew how to cook, she also worked as a chef and ran her own whole-food cooking school. Just when she'd enrolled for another degree (this time in psychology), she stumbled upon a creative writing course, and thought about becoming a writer because it was the type of job she could do in her pajamas. She is currently doing her master's in creative writing at Melbourne University, which she could quite possibly never finish. This is her first book.

everything hanging out. It sure did seem that, for such a tiny little thing, a baby really turned a person's life upside down.

Dad was cooking tuna pasta. "Want to help me whip up a salad, Sunny? There's a bag of mixed greens in the fridge, and an avocado that needs using."

"Sure," I said, opening the fridge door. It was looking like a proper fridge again. There was even soda. I washed the salad leaves, put them in the spinner and pulled and pulled the cord that made it whiz around. And I realized that I didn't feel that way anymore, all spinned up and whirling about like when the wind whips you up on those blustery days. It felt as though all my insides had slowed down and I didn't have anything to worry about anymore. I could just get back to thinking about inventions—like how to make a poem out of one of Flora's tiny baby sneezes before they got so big they were just like mine.

Just some of the naughty, disgusting and undignified things Willow did:

1. Clawed at the tiny hole in the couch and stuck her snout inside.
2. Pulled the clean sheets off the line, rolled on them and stuffed them into her kennel.
3. Picked up a stinking rotting dead water rat at the beach.
4. Pretended she was deaf and refused to drop it.
5. Rolled in the dead water rat.
6. Ran at high speed with the dead water rat toward a group of toddlers.
7. Completely trampled the children's sand castle while they screamed hysterically.
8. Dumped the dead water rat on the children's towels.
9. Barked at the children's mother, who was trying to shoo her away.
10. Laughed at me when I told her to sit.
11. Knocked over the kitchen bin and spread the rubbish all the way down the hall.
12. Put an empty dog food package in Mum's bed.
13. Stole Mum's tango shoes and buried one.
14. Stole my stuffed monkey and almost chewed the tail off.
15. Chewed the lapel off one of Mum's friend's leather jackets.
16. Chewed the antenna off the phone.
17. Ate one corner off nearly every cushion in the house.
18. Rolled in possum poo.
19. Ate possum poo.
20. Dug up Mum's stolen tango shoe, chewed the heel off and left it in Mum's bed.
21. Ate Mum's push-up bra in two.

Acknowledgments

This book was made extra possible thanks to:

Stephanie, Ondine and Tarquin Charlesworth for lend[ing a] hand with props, pizzas and cups of tea. Ava Clifforth fo[r be]ing the most excited person about my book, and for [her] handwritten contributions. The delightful Al Pal for [as] many phone calls as eleven-year-olds. Simonne, Nicki, [...] Munz, Kathryn, Al Pal, Guff, Emily, Foxy, Joanna, Jofie [and] Vivienne for your extraordinary friendship and enorm[ous] emotional support in my bleakest moments (that was the [new] me—please don't cash your credits in all at once). Ant[...] Jach, who noticed I had slunk away from uni and forced [me] to come back. Rosalind Price for giving me a break and [be]lieving in me. Susannah Chambers for her inspired and [ex]acting editorial assistance. The girls at Shabby club—J[o,] Ritchie, Tina and Kristi—thanks for the champers. Jonatha[n] Joh and Paul Chiodo for helping me with very importa[nt] transitions, Joe Connor and Jen Livingston for their artist[ic] support, Bill Roberts for alerting me to the fact that my do[g] was depressed, and Ian Lesser for being the most softhearte[d] and funniest criminal in town.

SEP 0 9 2010

.MAR 1 8 2009

everything hanging out. It sure did seem that, for such a tiny little thing, a baby really turned a person's life upside down.

Dad was cooking tuna pasta. "Want to help me whip up a salad, Sunny? There's a bag of mixed greens in the fridge, and an avocado that needs using."

"Sure," I said, opening the fridge door. It was looking like a proper fridge again. There was even soda. I washed the salad leaves, put them in the spinner and pulled and pulled the cord that made it whiz around. And I realized that I didn't feel that way anymore, all spinned up and whirling about like when the wind whips you up on those blustery days. It felt as though all my insides had slowed down and I didn't have anything to worry about anymore. I could just get back to thinking about inventions— like how to make a poem out of one of Flora's tiny baby sneezes before they got so big they were just like mine.

Just some of the naughty, disgusting and undignified things Willow did:

1. Clawed at the tiny hole in the couch and stuck her snout inside.
2. Pulled the clean sheets off the line, rolled on them and stuffed them into her kennel.
3. Picked up a stinking rotting dead water rat at the beach.
4. Pretended she was deaf and refused to drop it.
5. Rolled in the dead water rat.
6. Ran at high speed with the dead water rat toward a group of toddlers.
7. Completely trampled the children's sand castle while they screamed hysterically.
8. Dumped the dead water rat on the children's towels.
9. Barked at the children's mother, who was trying to shoo her away.
10. Laughed at me when I told her to sit.
11. Knocked over the kitchen bin and spread the rubbish all the way down the hall.
12. Put an empty dog food package in Mum's bed.
13. Stole Mum's tango shoes and buried one.
14. Stole my stuffed monkey and almost chewed the tail off.
15. Chewed the lapel off one of Mum's friend's leather jackets.
16. Chewed the antenna off the phone.
17. Ate one corner off nearly every cushion in the house.
18. Rolled in possum poo.
19. Ate possum poo.
20. Dug up Mum's stolen tango shoe, chewed the heel off and left it in Mum's bed.
21. Ate Mum's push-up bra in two.

ACKNOWLEDGMENTS

This book was made extra possible thanks to:

Stephanie, Ondine and Tarquin Charlesworth for lending a hand with props, pizzas and cups of tea. Ava Clifforth for being the most excited person about my book, and for her handwritten contributions. The delightful Al Pal for our many phone calls as eleven-year-olds. Simonne, Nicki, Jen Munz, Kathryn, Al Pal, Guff, Emily, Foxy, Joanna, Jofie and Vivienne for your extraordinary friendship and enormous emotional support in my bleakest moments (that was the old me—please don't cash your credits in all at once). Antoni Jach, who noticed I had slunk away from uni and forced me to come back. Rosalind Price for giving me a break and believing in me. Susannah Chambers for her inspired and exacting editorial assistance. The girls at Shabby club—Jen Ritchie, Tina and Kristi—thanks for the champers. Jonathan, Joh and Paul Chiodo for helping me with very important transitions, Joe Connor and Jen Livingston for their artistic support, Bill Roberts for alerting me to the fact that my dog was depressed, and Ian Lesser for being the most softhearted and funniest criminal in town.

MARION ROBERTS was born in Melbourne, Australia, where she still lives today. When she was young, she loved to sew and make her own clothes, so believed she was destined to become a fashion designer. Instead, she found herself studying science, alternative medicine, and psychotherapy, which wasn't such a helpful combination for a job in the fashion industry. She worked as a naturopath and counselor, and because she also knew how to cook, she also worked as a chef and ran her own whole-food cooking school. Just when she'd enrolled for another degree (this time in psychology), she stumbled upon a creative writing course, and thought about becoming a writer because it was the type of job she could do in her pajamas. She is currently doing her master's in creative writing at Melbourne University, which she could quite possibly never finish. This is her first book.